Fight or Die

From the corner of his eye, he saw Lily leave her post and run toward Maybel, screaming, "Maybel's hit."

Giving Francine a quick glance, Blackwood saw her face was set, her eyes narrow slits. "Come on you red devils." Her rifle was held to her shoulder at the ready.

Two warriors burst forth to his right followed by the other two on the left. Their whooping cries filled the air.

Blackwood jumped quickly to the area Lily left vacant, his rifle spitting lead to cover the move. Rolling behind a large dead log, he heard the near whiz of a bullet, then felt a burning sensation along his shoulder. He gave it little attention. A brave was nearly on top of him. Raising his gun to fire, he saw the Indian go down; one of the girls had tagged him.

When the three remaining warriors moved hell-bent out of rifle range, Blackwood called to the girls, "Hold your fire!"

BLACKWOOD

BLACKWOOD

B.J. PEVERLEY

PAGEANT BOOKS

PAGEANT BOOKS
225 Park Avenue South
New York, New York 10003

Cover artwork by Hiram Richardson

Printed in the U.S.A.

First Pageant Books printing: March, 1989

10 9 8 7 6 5 4 3 2 1

To Dr. Ronald Berez

HISTORICAL NOTE

To keep the story in its proper historical perspective the word gun is not used. That term didn't come into common usage in this country until the late 1800s.

BLACKWOOD

Chapter One

HE'D COME FROM the north, not riding hard but keeping a steady pace. Reining to a halt by a stream on a tree-covered foothill, he lifted himself in the saddle to scan the area. As his eyes moved to the east and saw the view obscured by a dense stand of trees, a frown pinched his brow. Man and horse stood quiet, as if listening for the sprigs of spring grass to pop through the warming earth. Slowly, the firm, fixed look of concentration dissolved from his face and he stepped to the ground releasing the reins. The piebald dipped his head for a cool drink.

The dark-clad man dropped to his knees beside the stream, untied the neckerchief from around his neck, laid aside his wide-brim hat, shucked his black shirt, and splashed the icy water over his broad muscular shoulders. A few drops of cold water clung to the dark mat on his breastbone, others rolled down his arms as he washed a face that looked as if it had been chiseled from granite.

Rising to his over six foot of height, he stretched, retrieved his hat, and beat the dust from his trousers. After thrusting his arms into the shirtsleeves he dug the makings from a pocket. While building the cigarette, he sighed, promising himself meat, and a cup of good strong coffee, for supper. The pony, ignoring him, continued to nibble at the tender shoots of grass.

He leaned against a tree to finish his smoke and give his horse the rest it sorely needed. He had been in the saddle since dawn and where the sun was now, surrounded by puffy white clouds in a blue sky, he knew it must be almost noon.

As he took a long pull on the cigarette, his thoughts traveled back in time to the outlaws who raided the Blackwood Ranch. They had murdered his mother, father, and raped his sister, leaving her for dead. His sister, Leeann, survived, but her mind had been damaged. A compassionate aunt had taken her East to care for her.

Blackwood was a grave, trail-weary man and had searched for these desperadoes longer than he cared to think about. But time meant nothing to him where they were concerned; he had vowed to see each one brought to justice, if it took a lifetime.

Through the years, on the trail, he had learned many valuable lessons. He read sign as well as an Apache and recognized the cry of any animal. He handled a knife or drew a six-shooter with more speed and accuracy than most, to name but a few of the abilities that had saved his life more than once.

Shaking off the past he heard a faint creak, squeak, creak, coming from the East. His foot ground the cigarette into the earth, one hand dropped to the leather on his hip, the other reached for the reins. Man and horse moved back into the shadows. His cool green eyes narrowed to slits beneath hooded lids, intent and alert.

"Damn," he growled, but elected to wait and see, then decide if it was best to backtrack and ride wide to avoid an encounter.

His trail south had been through the Bitterroot highlands and he had grown accustomed to the scant concealment the trees afforded. Now he must cross the great expanse of open rolling hills of grass before him, directly in the path of the intruder.

He was in Indian territory. Although there was no real trouble as yet, it was only a matter of time. A few hot-blooded young braves would raid and plunder, but the true worry was the outlaws and rough troublemakers who came to the territory at the first whisper of gold. Some prospectors were lazy, and when they realized the hard work involved in mining they turned to thievery. They often killed other miners, homesteaders, and travelers in small wagon trains, for a few meager possessions.

The plop-plop-plop of hooves pounding the earth and the creak of the wheels told Blackwood more than four animals were pulling an overloaded wagon. As the sound of the strain the wagon was under grew louder he could detect the voices of women. When the wagon slowly groaned its way around the knoll, he gasped, and stared in disbelief. Damned if it wasn't the strangest sight. A more dilapidated wagon he had never seen, pulled by six of the most handsome Missouri mules he'd ever hoped to view.

He counted six women but no men. One woman was driving the team, the others were scattered about the open field. They were skipping, singing, and one was even picking wild flowers.

"Well, I'll be go-to-hell," he sputtered. "You would think they were back East frolicking in their own backyard." He swore wearily again and wondered what miracle had seen them this far into the territory.

His eyes cut to the wagon again. It couldn't be, but sure as hell, that was ruffles flapping on the sides of the wagon. With a closer look he realized the ruffles were attached to women's petticoats and bloomers stretched across the top.

Chapter Two

BLACKWOOD SLUMPED IN his saddle, staring moodily at the women. He knew he had to alert those foolish females to the perils they should be prepared to meet in this part of the country.

Slowly, he started down the gentle slope. "Easy boy," he spoke softly to the piebald. "We don't want to cause a ruckus. We want them to see we mean no harm before we get too close."

The wagon stopped. The girls ran to gather beside it, excitedly whispering, as they watched him draw nearer.

When he halted before them it became very still. Even the breeze seemed to be holding its breath.

He touched his hat, surveyed their faces, hid his surprise at coming across a bevy of beauties, and said, "Howdy, ladies."

"Y'all by yourself?" questioned a dark-haired charmer in a red satin dress that shimmered in the bright sun. She appeared to be a little older than the others and placed herself in front as if to declare she was in charge.

"Yes, ma'am," he said, catching the slow drawl of her deep Southern accent.

"He don't look threatenin' to me, Maybel," the girl holding the mules' traces determined, as her deep blue eyes roamed over his broad shoulders and slim hips. Her gaze also took in the cut of his clothes, as well as the fancy black rig with the fine piece of black and white horse-flesh underneath.

The dark-haired woman in the red dress contemplated for a moment, then nodded. "I'm Maybel, this here girl handlin' the team with the quick judgment is Lily."

"Folks call me Blackwood," he said, responding with a nod.

Maybel flung her hand out in a dramatic gesture and introduced the other girls.

"Honey," a low, husky voice cooed.

Blackwood twisted in the saddle to give his full attention to the girl who made the dovelike sound. He found himself gazing at a hazel-eyed blonde, long on looks. With a start Blackwood realized, but without a whisper of emotion showing, it wouldn't do to look too deep in those beautiful eyes. They were stone-cold dead.

"Ah'm Francine," she said in a slow drawl. "We're fixin' to stop pretty quick an have a bite to eat. Won't y'all join us?"

"Much obliged, ma'am." He shook his head. "But I only stopped to warn you about the harm that can come to you in this territory. The sight I saw from the ridge yonder told me you were addle-headed pilgrims an could use a bit of advice."

"Aw, come on, surely you can take time to have a bite to eat with us," several voices chimed, ignoring his cutting remark.

"Everyone has to eat and we have plenty,

don't we, girls?" Lily, the muleskinner, coaxed, then flashed a sour look at Francine.

Aw hell, what could one or two hours really matter? He felt welcome—or almost. The only exception seemed to be the girl Maybel had introduced as her daughter. Wilma was frowzy with stringy, wild hair. She stood slumped over, silent, head bent, and shuffling her feet. A most unpleasant looking girl.

"Reckon it wouldn't hurt none to get a good meal under my belt." Blackwood slowly smiled.

"You can tell us about them dangers, soon's we find a place to stop," said Lily as she flicked a bull whip to urge the mules forward.

He nudged his horse to move leisurely beside the wagon. Moving along at a slow pace soon set Blackwood to thinking. He smiled, but it wasn't a pleasant smile as his thoughts traveled back to the man who had put him on this trail. The man's name was Roscoe Watts and Blackwood had trailed him for over two months to the North Fork country. Watts was one of the men who took part in the raid on the Blackwood Ranch. By the time Blackwood caught up with him, Watts and three henchmen had tried treeing the small community of Marnet, north of Sock Creek. The men in the small town and the ranchers in the outlying area banded together, captured them, and sentenced all four to be hung.

Blackwood visited the jail to question Watts. Watts talked freely about the many outlaw bands he rode with in scattered parts of the country. Finding it tiresome listening to him brag, Blackwood turned the conversation to the raids Watts had participated in, south of the Brazos. When he described the Blackwood Ranch, Blackwood held his rage in check while attempting to extract the names of the gang members who had been with him. The outlaws now in jail with Watts said they had never been near the Brazos. Through steadfast questioning, Watts confessed he hardly knew the men he rode with but there was one he'd seen in Fort Boise less than a month ago.

"Don't rightly know his name," Watts said. "But everyone called him Sandy because of his wild sandy hair and beard."

When Blackwood knew he had gotten all the information Watts would give he told him who he was. Fearful, Watts took a step backward then cringed to the back of his cell.

Blackwood tarried only long enough to see Watts hung. Now he was in a hurry to get to Fort Boise before Sandy's trail got too cold.

The pretty redheaded gal walking beside the wagon broke through Blackwood's thoughts. She was shouting to the muleskinner—"Lily, do y'all think you could get the wagon over by that stream?"—while pushing back in place the damp red tendrils that were beginning to cling to her face. "It would be nice to eat yonder under that tree and get out of this sun for a spell." She tilted her head questioningly toward Lily.

"Sho', Cora. No problem with the mules, but betcha this broken-down wagon will give me a heap of trouble," Lily answered, with a hard accent on the word "wagon," and a cold look at Francine.

"Oh, Lily, you've no call to put all the blame on Francine." Cora tried to reason with her. "Remember when we bought the mules, Maybel, Jenny, 'n Wilma went with Francine to pick out the wagon." Reading the look on Lily's face Cora sighed, shrugged her shoulders, and gave up.

Blackwood thought Cora looked a little out of place in the company of Maybel, Francine, and Lily. Those three had the look of dyed-in-the-wool good-time girls. Glancing again at the women, his gaze settled on Jenny. She was an absolute contrast. The shy young lady was definitely out of place. She was a fresh-faced youngster, with straight sandy hair reaching to her waist. She couldn't have been more than fourteen or maybe fifteen. The mass of drooping purple grass widows, yellowbells, and Indian paintbrush she held in her arms looked right with the face, but wrong with the bright, gaudy, obviously cast-off dress she was wearing.

Curiosity getting the best of Blackwood he dismounted to walk with Cora and try to pick up some information. "Those two have a fight?" he questioned with a nod in Lily's direction.

"Oh, if it twern't one thing it would be another." Cora gave a stretched, thin sigh. "Lily
grew up on a farm an' she knows animals an'
such, but anyway those two gals just don't like
each other." She looked up at him and asked
candidly, "What you doin' in these parts?"

"I'm heading toward Fort Boise. Where are
you ladies bound?" He sidestepped her direct
question.

"We're goin' the same direction," she exclaimed. "We could travel together."

"Well, I'm in pretty much of a hurry."

"This creakin' ol' wagon would hold you up
some," she said, as if reading his thoughts.

"How long you been puttin' up with it?"

"We had it 'bout a month or so. First thing
happened was we got in a wind storm and the
top got torn off. 'Course, it weren't no good to
begin with. Had a big hole in it," she scoffed.
"Jenny sewed that top. Not much better, but
covers our stuff. Lily sez won't last no longer 'n
a snowball in Hades, if we run into bad
weather." She stopped to catch her breath.

He nodded in agreement. "I'm afraid Lily's
right. This far north is rougher going, but water
is easier to come by. Where you ladies from?" he
asked. "I know it's the South but what part?"

"We's from New Orleans, exceptin' Jenny. We
picked her up 'long the way. She lost her maw,
the last of her folks. So she come with us to
work.

"What? She's a...?" He cast her a probing look.

Cora hesitated, reticent. With a mischievous look on her face she glanced at him then began to stir restlessly under the impact of his gaze. Letting out a nervous titter she quickly continued. "Oh, no, not the same work we do. Maybel don't think she's ready. Too young. She just fetch, and carry, you know, wash, clean, an such."

Changing the subject, he said, "That wagon is in sorry shape," and watched as Lily guided it under the tree. "There's a minin' camp 'bout two days' ride from here. Maybe you should go by that way, an' see if you could get a stronger top for it. Sooner or later you're bound to run into bad weather."

"A minin' camp. Maybel will be happy to hear that. She sez there's lots of lonesome men and gold in them camps." She quickly moved away, anxious to give Maybel this news.

After sopping up the last of the juice he set the plate aside, and built himself a cigarette. "I want you to remember what I told you about protectin' yourselves against the outlaws an other dangers in this territory." Taking a long pull on the cigarette, he added, "I surely do thank you ladies, that was a right good meal." He patted his lean belly, displaying appreciation. "Now don't you go forgetting how to get to that minin' camp. Is there anything I can do for you before I leave?" As they shook their heads, he stood to move toward his horse. "Well, I best get on. I want to cover a good deal of ground before dark."

As he swung into the saddle Maybel called out, "Please wait, I'd like one more word with you."

The girls bunched and began to talk low among themselves.

"I'm sorry, ladies, I've run out of time. Gotta make tracks." He was impatient to push on.

"Please, just one more second," Maybel called.

He heard one of the girls shout, "You're out-voted," and noticed Wilma vigorously shaking her head.

The mystery was solved when Maybel came to where he impatiently waited, and said, "Black-wood, we have a deal for you. If you'll guide us to Fort Boise, we'll pay for the service."

Well, for crap sakes, he thought, is that what all that jabber was about? Damnation, they had found their way this far. He studied Maybel, trying to hide his aggravation.

Shaking his head he started to wheel the pie-bald about, when Maybel said, "I wish you would think on it. Three hundred dollars sure is a mess of money to turn down."

"Like I said, I'm in pretty much of a hurry." He scowled. Then thoughts of Leeann's doctor bills and living expenses crossed his mind.

"Don't leave, I'll be right back." Maybel hurried the short distance to the other girls and the whispering began again.

"Forget it, Maybel." He was fighting the urge to accept.

If he guided that old, broken-down wagon, the trip could take weeks instead of days. But if he rode off, chances were he would come back. It wasn't in him to step around this and ride off, knowing that without someone to guide and help them, there was a slim chance they would survive. And the three hundred would come in handy.

Maybel came bustling up to him before he could dismount and accept. She said, "Awright, we'uns can make it four hundred but I wantcha to know that's our limit."

"Before we complete the deal let's get our heads together and make sure we understand each other." He dismounted and led Maybel to join the others.

Blackwood laid out the rules. First, he was to receive half the money now and the balance at the end of the trail. "You're to follow my orders, and at no time are you to stray more than a few feet from the wagon." He explained how easy he could have picked off Lily, used the wagon as cover while he cut them down, even if they'd had weapons.

Discovering they had nails, ropes, and other materials to repair the wagon, he suggested they use the balance of the day to work on the wagon and move out come early morning. When he mentioned they should change their bright dresses for something a little more sedate, which couldn't be seen for miles, they moaned their displeasure.

"In fact," he said, "it would be better if you dressed like men. Anyone would think twice before attackin' seven men." Looking at Wilma he caught a menacing, hostile look on her face. "You talk it over, those are my terms." He turned to move out of earshot.

"No need, we agree." Maybel answered for everyone, and all but Wilma nodded their heads.

His gaze narrowed, and a foreboding came over him as he looked at Wilma. "Do you agree, Wilma?"

She hung her head and mumbled, "We're in the middle of nowhere an' nobody will listen to me." She shrugged her shoulders, saying, "I guess so."

"I can't accept that. It's either you do or you don't. I won't put up with problems after we get under way." He frowned.

Maybel gave Wilma a poke in the ribs and a measured look. "Wilma agrees," Maybel ground out.

"Awright." Wilma's voice was flat.

He looked at her again and read naked hate in her eyes. He could not understand why she had taken such an immediate dislike to him and decided it would bear watching.

"It would do well for all of you to remember

what you agreed to, then everything will go smooth," he stated doggedly.

Maybel handed Blackwood two small leather bags. "You'll take gold, won'tcha?" she asked. "Each of those pokes is worth a hundred, so I'll owe you two more when we reach Fort Boise."

Blackwood weighed each sack in the palm of his hand. "This one seems a bit skimpy." He tossed the bag to her, his steady gaze holding her as he ran his hand across the back of his neck.

"Maybe it seems that way 'cause the other one is a trifle heavy." Maybel took a step closer, giving him a clear view down the front of her low-cut bodice.

It had been a while since he'd been with a woman and he felt a stirring begin in his loins. Her full, ripe breasts looked as if they wanted to spill out into his hands.

A small smile touched his lips. He knew the move had been to distract him. "On the whole, I'd say more than a trifle short." His eyes then drifted to peruse the other women as he continued. "This is gonna be a long trail. How about we come up with another way to make up the difference?" The words with his expression said he would like a girl at his beck and call at all times.

His eyes continued to rake over the other women, causing Maybel to puff up. "Ah'm afraid the shortage wouldn't quite pay the price. My girls are expensive." She turned pink when she realized her statement was an admission of trying to cheat him.

"Then just what do you propose we do about the shortage?" The person to get the best of Blackwood in a deal was yet to come along, he wasn't about to let it start now.

Seeing it was a no-win situation, she said, "I'll bring it to you after supper." She smiled to take the sting out and continued, "I jus' hate it when I lose." She flipped around to walk away, but not before he saw the look in her eyes, which said, it isn't so bad losing to some. He felt it was possible he might get something extra, when she brought him the bag of dust tonight.

Chapter Three

EVERYONE SET TO doing their fair share of the chores.

Jenny strung a rope from the wagon to the tree, to hang laundry. Each time Blackwood walked by he dodged wet garments.

"Damn it all to hell," he bellowed. "Jenny, get this damn rope down. Every time I pass this side of the wagon I get slapped in the face with a pair of wet drawers." Not yet ready to accept the course of events, he was irritable enough to rail at anyone.

Cora started to chuckle. Her giggle seemed to convey an amusing picture to the other girls and they burst into laughter; even Wilma's face lost its usual scowl.

"Don't get your dander up. They have to dry," defended Jenny.

"Then spread 'em out there on the tall grass, in the sun." Blackwood gestured impatiently toward the tall green carpet surrounding them. "To fix this damn wagon I have to be able to get around it." He frowned, ignoring their laughter.

By the time the wagon was fixed to Blackwood's satisfaction, the shadows had grown long and supper was almost ready. Not wanting any surprises while he was enjoying his coffee, he climbed into his saddle to again give the area the once-over.

Later, he took a last pull on his cigarette then flipped the butt into the open fire. "It was a fine meal," he complimented and drained his coffee cup. "We best turn in pretty quick, we'll be getting a early start in the morning."

Jenny rose to refill his cup, but he waved her away.

"Well, I'm not goin' to bed till I get a bath," she declared as she set the pot down.

"I found a pond and already took a bath," Wilma said.

"Where is it?" asked Jenny.

"In them trees up yonder a ways." Wilma pointed upstream as she moved into the firelight, rubbing her wet hair.

Several girls shrieked and pandemonium followed as they laughed, squealed, and scrambled around for soap, towels, and clean garments.

Damned if this job ain't going to be one of my bigger mistakes, Blackwood scowled.

"For Christ's sake, shut up." He yelled to get their attention. "You're makin' enough noise to wake the dead. Sound travels out here, an' if someone is skulking around out there, this loud carryin'-on will lead them right here to camp. An' how many of you are keen on not livin' to see the sunrise if they ain't friendlies? Get your bath, but be damn quiet about it," he peevishly warned.

Subdued, they quietly filed out of camp, headed toward the hidden pond. He was aware he'd scared the hell out of them, just as he'd intended.

Immediately after the girls left Wilma stated, "I'm tired." By chance Blackwood looked up, square into her cold obsidian eyes, and saw no fear in her hostile gaze. His skin began to crawl and the thought slid to him, there's something haywire about this gal.

Wilma was bedded down under the wagon before the girls piled back into camp.

As Maybel moved to pass Blackwood, he laid his hand on her arm. "I'm gonna wash, then bed down up there." He gestured toward a ridge above the campsite.

"You think I'd forget?" she purred and gave him a silky smile. "I'll find you."

Maybel's eyes followed the big man in black. This was one man whose thinker wasn't puny. He didn't quite have the look of a pistoleer, but somehow she knew he could be just as deadly. She was hypnotized by the prominence of the muscles across his broad shoulders and the power emerging from him, as his lithe, catlike stride carried him out of camp.

He made his way to the small catch basin in the narrow glade and stood silent, listening to the night noises. Kneeling, he plunged his hand in the water, swishing it around. It was cold, but he decided his clothes could use a wash. He shed his dusty black boots, hat, and carefully hung his holster on an easily accessible low limb. Peeling off his clothes, he sank into the frigid water.

After the chill of the water, he felt warmth in the soft blackness of the night when he pulled himself from the pond and stretched. Hunkering at the water's edge he washed his clothes. He doused them several times to rinse out the soap and was about to wring out the water when he heard a disturbance behind him. What the... can't be Maybel. Cursing himself for being carelessly engrossed he quickly rolled to the balls of his feet. Stealthily palming his shooting iron he patiently waited, crouched in the deep shadows.

Chapter Four

AN UNDETERMINED LENGTH of time passed while a great amount of thrashing about in the underbrush occurred. A large black body with a white blaze, and a splash of white across his chest, broke into the small clearing. Reaching for the piebald's halter Blackwood did not relax. He knew the stallion would not wander this far, he was too well trained. Someone had led him.

He caught a faint sound of something moving toward the direction of the camp. By the time he maneuvered into position to get a clear view of the path and the wagon there were three girls milling about. The distance made it impossible to tell if one had just joined the other two.

Chill bumps rose on his naked body as he stood collecting himself and trying to puzzle out the whys and hows his horse had made it to the pond. The pony would come to him from a few yards away for a stroke or a rub, but never this far without being summoned. Maybe the horse wandered toward the wagon and one of the women brought him up here. For what purpose? He remembered he had firmly secured the reins to a branch on the up side of the creek. He knew the piebald could perform many feats, but untying himself from a secure knot wasn't one of them.

Blackwood had a gut feeling this was someone's way of telling him to get on his horse and ride.

Strapping the six-shooter around his naked body he jammed his feet in the boots and retrieved his wet clothes. Fumbling around he found his lye soap, then picked up the piebald's reins and headed toward his bedroll.

"I'll be damned if I'll let a woman run me off," he told himself as he made his way through the brush.

Removing his boots he pulled on clean long johns, then eased himself down on his bedroll. Raising his arms over his head, his hands caressed his rifle before pushing it under the blanket and saddlebags he used to rest his head on.

His clothes were stretched out to dry and the stallion hobbled when the noise Maybel was making, trying to get up the hill, became frenzied.

"Blackwood, where'n hell are you?" she called softly.

"Over here, just keep straight on." He kept the amusement out of his voice.

"Dammit, why the hell did you bed down way up here?" she complained.

"I can keep my eye on everything down there." He waved his hand toward the lowland.

Below was a clear view in all directions. The moon was high, bathing the trees and shrubs in shimmering silver. The shallow stream glittered as it bubbled its way down the slope between the trees, then rambled along separating him and the wagon.

"The sights I've seen since I've left home fairly take my breath away." She sighed then turned to look at him thoughtfully.

He patted the bedroll inviting her to sit down. "You have somethin' for me?" he asked. "I like to take care of business right off, leaves more time for other things." He ran his hand over her shoulder and down her arm.

She dug in the pocket of the flowing black robe and handed him a small pouch. Blackwood dropped it in the saddlebag.

She began to fiddle with the buttons on his long johns. "Where do you come from?" She leaned over him and fleetingly pressed her lips to his.

"Across the Bitterroot." He less than half answered her question and not at all of his origin, as he began to nibble on her bottom lip.

She now had several buttons undone and was stroking him across the dark mat on his chest. "You known a lot of women?"

He felt a tightening in his loins each time her soft fluttery strokes crossed his nipples. "Enough to know they make it a pleasure to be a man." He tightened his arms around her and rolled her on her back.

She pulled at him and raised her lips. He hungrily drank in her kisses and felt her tremble as her body writhed in his embrace.

His hand found the bow holding the robe together. Giving it a tug he brushed aside the folds of material. In the half shadow he saw the only clothing she wore; a bright red garter belt and thigh-high black silk hose.

He ran his hand over her silky thigh and up her rib cage to her full firm breasts and down again as he explored her lush body. His fingers traced the softness of her breasts and their rigid points.

As he moved over her velvety moans came from her throat. Her silky thighs caressed his sides.

Suddenly a piercing scream penetrated the night, followed by shouts and loud angry voices.

Chapter Five

BEFORE THE RACKET reached Maybel, Blackwood was alert and crouched beside the bedroll. The rifle was gripped in his hand, at the ready.

"What the...?" Maybel sat up with a befuddled look.

Quickly drawing on damp trousers he strapped the leather cartridge belt around his lean hips and pointed toward the wagon. "What the hell's goin' on down there?"

The pale moon gave enough light to see two figures going at it ass over-tea kettle on the ground. Their arms were thrashing and their voices were raised in loud, angry shrieks. The other three girls contributed to the noise and confusion by shouting and hopping about.

What was happening dawned on Maybel. She jumped up, rearranged her clothing, and poked her loose strands of hair back in place. "It's got to be Lily and Francine. Damn...damn them," she sputtered as her voice mounted in anger. "I sho' wish to hell them two would get along."

Blackwood shook his head in disgust. If he didn't feel responsible for their safety, he'd let them fight it out, but as it was, he shrugged and motioned to Maybel to follow. "Come on, we best get there before they kill each other." Not stopping to put on his boots, he slipped and skidded down the slope, the rocks and brambles taking their toll on his feet. Maybel scrambled behind him.

As they forded the shallow, narrow stream Maybel angrily shouted, "Stop, you fools. Grab Lily, Blackwood. Jenny, Cora, help me with Francine."

"Why the hell are you brawlin'?" Blackwood growled, pinning Lily's arms at her sides while Maybel and Jenny held Francine.

"That bitch..." Lily sputtered, pointing at

Francine. "That bitch...I was sound asleep an' she clouted me."

"I did no such thing," Francine hissed, struggling to get away from Maybel and Jenny. "I was asleep an' you attacked me for no reason."

"Why, you lyin', ugly bitch, I didn't touch you," Lily screeched, trying to get at Francine.

"'Nuff of this foolishness. You hear me?" shouted Maybel.

"Maybe I rolled over"—Cora's voice rose above the din—"an' accidently bashed against one of you." She looked contrite. "I was sleeping between you, remember?"

Giving Cora puzzled looks Francine and Lily fell quiet.

Blackwood glanced at Maybel in time to catch the grimace she cast Wilma and noted how Wilma shrugged her shoulders, giving Maybel a sly grin. When Wilma raised her head and saw Blackwood looking at her she quickly changed the expression to cold indifference.

"Didn't I warn you about all this caterwauling? For Christ's sake, just simmer down an' get back to bed." Blackwood didn't raise his voice, but it could be clearly heard in the sudden quiet. "Dawn will be here in short order an' every last one of you will wish you hadn't missed this sleep."

Jabbing her finger at Lily and Francine, Maybel said, "I want you two to stay away from one another. Blackwood an' I have finished our business." She slid Wilma a sideways glance. "So if I hear one more peep out of you, I'll be here to choke y'all down."

Blackwood gave Maybel a disgruntled glare and cussed every step of the way back to his bedroll, alone, totally unaware of the finely balanced silhouette he cast in the moonlight.

He woke before the first streak of gray announced the dawn. There was a crisp chill in the spring morning, the moon had set, and a clear, star-riddled sky met his eyes. Closing his eyes again he let his senses take over. His hearing told him there was a stirring in the camp, and sniffing, he caught the scent of coffee wafting through the air. Rolling out, he dressed in his seam-damp clothes, tied his bedroll in a neat bundle, and fastened it behind his saddle. Digging a rough towel from the saddlebag he headed toward the stream. The clicking sound he made with his tongue told the piebald to follow.

"My goodness, your clothes are wet," Jenny exclaimed, handing him a cup of coffee.

"Jus' around the edges, be dry before midday," Blackwood assured her.

"You'll be lucky if you don't catch your death." Jenny looked at him with concern.

Giving her a tolerant grin, he didn't comment.

It was a quiet time, with the exception of Jenny. The girls resented getting up early and had gone about the preparation of breaking camp with sullen faces, sleepy eyes, and glares at Jenny, because of her chattering.

The blush of morning was visible by the time the mules were hitched, the fire doused, and all were ready to move out.

When Lily climbed up on the seat to drive the team, Blackwood placed a rifle beside her, saying, "I got this out of your wagon. It's loaded. You know how to use it?" When she nodded he continued. "If you run into trouble fire off one shot. I'll just be up the trail a ways, won't take no time to get back to you."

After cautioning her to follow the marked path, he mounted and rode west. He was hugging foothills that had lofty snow-capped peaks towering in the background. Spread out to the south were endless rolling hills.

Having blazed the trail for some distance, he now scouted the region, keeping his eyes peeled. He was on the lookout for a suitable spot with water and good grass to rest the mules, and stop for the midday meal.

Topping a low rise Blackwood reined to a halt, studied the ground, and sniffed the air. It held a stench. He dismounted cautiously as a wispy column of smoke appeared above the next hill. With his rifle at the ready, he made his way to the rise. Drawing near the top he lay flat to peer over the hill. The smell and the sight made his stomach turn.

Picking his way, he moved down the hill to the smoldering remains of a wagon. Three bodies lay amid the ashes, a man, a woman, and a young boy. They had each been shot, their belongings plundered, then torched.

He circled the ill-fated wagon, finding sign two shod horses had come from the south, then left going east, toward the girls. He would come back later and take care of the burial. For now, it was a matter of getting back to the women without delay. Bolting into the saddle he gave the stallion its head.

When he drew close, knowing the wagon was below the next rise, he held back on the reins to slow the piebald. Riding easy over the knoll he approached with care.

Drawing near he saw two hard-faced men close to the girls' wagon. One wore a coonskin cap, the other a nondescript moth-eaten felt. Both wore filthy, well-worn clothing.

The wild-eyed gent wearing the coonskin cap had Francine trapped a few yards from the wagon. He rode in a circle around her, grabbing at her dress and giving a quick jerk. She ran first one way then the other, clutching at the fragments of her dress, trying to cover her body. Fifty yards or so away the man in the felt hat was almost bent double with laughter while holding a pistol on the other women.

As Blackwood slipped the thong from his pistol and moved steadily forward, he could see the girls' faces begin to change. Their pale, drawn expressions switched to one of greeting, but before they could speak he drawled, "Looks like you boys are havin' yourselves a little fun." His chiseled face was set and his green eyes were as cold as chips of ice.

Chapter Six

THE MAN IN the coonskin cap looked up and stopped circling Francine, but couldn't keep his eyes from straying back to her.

"Why you come sneakin' up on us, mister? Ya better just keep movin'." The words came from the grimy man in the felt hat. A sneer smeared its way across the lips of his hatchet face, while his attitude held an air of feeling sure he'd have his way. Blackwood decided to deal with him first.

Seemingly unconcerned Blackwood shrugged and made as if to ride off. Then, as if it were an afterthought, he settled back on his horse and asked, "By the way, have either of you gents run across a friend of mine, goes by the name of Sandy?" He started describing Sandy.

The man holding the six-shooter on the girls interrupted. "Never heard of him, we don't buddy up with anyone, nohow."

Blackwood held the eyes of the man. "Well, how about remembering if you saw a burned-out wagon back yonder?" He forced his lips to smile to disguise the hostility in his voice.

"Hell," guffawed the man near Francine. "See it? Those buggers put up a fight. But Ol' Sid an' me made short work of 'em." His manner and laugh tipped Blackwood to the fact the man was ruthless but a mighty slow thinker. This confirmed his decision to take care of Ol' Sid first.

"Shut up, Earl," Ol' Sid snapped as his eyes took in the piebald.

"I was jus'—" Earl started to explain.

"I said, shut ya mouth!" Sid grated as he continued to eye Blackwood's horse.

"Well, I best be gettin' on," Blackwood said, as he made up his mind to gamble, and wheeled the piebald about to go between Earl and Sid. Blackwood knew this had to be timed just right or, the second he was beyond Sid, he would have a hole in his back, and Sid would have a damn good stallion. With the pressure of his knees and a twitch of the reins Blackwood sent the stallion into a prancing gait. When the horse pranced barely behind Sid, Blackwood said, in a soft, almost inaudible voice, "You dirty, lousy son-of-a-bitch."

"What did ya say?" Sid whirled and that was his mistake. When he swung around, no longer pointing the pistol at the girls, Blackwood pulled the action on his six-shooter. There was an explosion, and the blood, from a hole in the middle of his forehead, trickled down between Sid's eyes.

With a flash Sid's pistol discharged. The bullet plowed a furrow in the turf as he fell to the ground.

Quickly Blackwood drew a bead on Earl, but Earl had his hands over his head screaming, "No! No! We was gonna share the girls with ya. I'll tell you what, I'll ride off quiet like an' you can have the girls."

"I can't leave the ladies to take you to the law, so it has to be done this way. You won't ever rough up any more girls, an' back there"— Blackwood slightly dipped his head in the direction of the burned-out wagon—"is the last family you will ever murder." With eyes narrowed and lips tight the peacemaker in his hand belched fire. When the bullet struck Earl in the chest he back-flipped off his horse.

"That was too quick for the bastard. He should've been made to suffer a passel more fo' what he done to me," Francine fumed and stomped to the wagon.

Lily glared at her. "If you hadn't run, jus' thinkin' of your own self, you wouldn't been caught out there alone. Besides, y'all heared what Blackwood said about that poor family out there. Should be feelin' sorry for them an' not yourself."

Francine shrugged and moved to enter the wagon. "Look at my dress, I gotta find somethin' to put on. Jenny, do you suppose this un could be mended?"

Lily slowly shook her head and muttered,

"Francine, you are no doubt the most self-centered bitch a person ever had the misfortune to know."

Their confrontation being of little importance to them, the other girls ignored it.

"Landsakes! Blackwood," Maybel cried. "I sho' was happy to see you. I was sure my life was ended. When you came over that hill it was a glorious sight."

With eyes as round as saucers and a catch in her voice, Jenny said, "I was so scared."

Wilma pacified her, repeating, "It's awright, it's over now."

Cora stammered, "Oh . . . dear, don't you think we should've . . . taken that one"—she indicated Earl—"to a sheriff or . . . somethin' . . . instead of jus' . . . killin' 'im?"

"You are out of your head, girl," Lily barked at Cora. "Look around, don't you know where we'uns are? Don' waste your sympathy on that trash."

"I know, but—" Cora began, as she raked at her hair with her fingers, trying to smooth the unruly curls back from her face.

"That's enough, yuh hear?" Maybel interrupted. "Justice was served right here." Pointing toward the ground she stressed the word "here," turned to the other girls, saying, "Did y'all hear me?" They nodded and she continued. "I want you to remember that, an' say no more 'bout it."

Each girl, with eyes trained on Blackwood,

was visibly shaken and began to chatter nervously.

Holstering his six-shooter Blackwood sat very still atop the stallion. Rage boiled inside him as tormenting memories of his family, sparked off by the sight of the murdered three, crowded in on him. He knew Earl or Sid would not have hesitated to back-shoot him and he felt no pangs of conscience over their death. But, killing always left him with a strange hollow feeling.

Holding himself in check he rode the few yards to Earl's pony and led him back to the girls, saying roughly, "For God's sake, all this prattle is enough to drive a man crazy. Here, unsaddle this horse an' turn him loose. He's a scrub mustang. He'll make out." Taking the reins of Sid's horse he led the animal to the rear of the wagon. "Take off this one's saddle an' put it in the wagon and fix him to the back here."

Moving up to ride point again, but only a few yards ahead of the mules, he turned his head slightly, and hurled over his shoulder in a much harsher tone, "Get that wagon amovin'. We ain't got all day, let's roll." Thinking better of his irate action, he wheeled his horse about to face them, and in a moderate voice speculated, "Maybe up the trail a ways we'll find a couple of trees, good water, an' grass where we can rest a bit."

"Don' you think we should bury them?" Cora whispered, sidling up to Maybel.

"Why?" Maybel frowned. "I sho'nuff don't

know what to think about you, Cora." She shook her head. "You know animals would just dig them up again. Forget it an' get in the wagon."

Each girl rode or walked beside the wagon warily, silently engrossed in their own thoughts.

They had traveled well past the noon hour when a grassy knoll gave way to a dark cluster of trees. Beneath the trees was a large Conestoga and four saddled horses. Out a ways, near a stream, four massive oxen busily grazed.

Chapter Seven

IT WAS A peaceful scene, but knowing things were not always as they appeared, Blackwood held up his hand, signaling Lily to stop the wagon. Riding back to the girls he said, "All of you stay here, close together. I don't expect trouble but you never know. If you hear shots, get over that hill, yonder, an' prepare to protect yourselves."

Walking his horse toward the large wagon he called out, "Halloooo, in camp."

Five brawny, fair-haired men stepped forward with rifles held easy in their hands. A man at the far right motioned and shouted, "Come on in."

On closer inspection, Blackwood noted, four of the men were young and the one giving him leave to enter camp was more gray than fair-haired. The eldest looked to be about fifty while the youngest was maybe nineteen. Each was a mirror image of the other, big open faces with deep blue eyes holding a direct, keen interest. They were dressed in the garb of farmers. Their rifles were shiny new and of a type Blackwood had never seen. Smiles crossed their faces as they greeted him with nods, which made them seem friendly.

One of the young men said, "That's an odd-looking wagon."

" 'Light, stranger," the eldest said, and shot a reproving glance at the young man who made the remark. "Your family in the wagon?"

"No," he stated, dismounting, but from habit kept his right hand free. "If you don't mind we would like to rest here, an' let the mules feed." Seeing their genial but curious glances toward the wagon he felt it right to mention the girls. "I'm guiding trail-green fancy ladies to Fort Boise."

One of the men chuckled and nudged the one next to him. "Now if that don't beat all. Women!"

The gray-haired man growled, "John!" and glared so threateningly it wiped the big grin off the young man's face. He turned to Blackwood. "Fancy women? Well, that being the case we got us a problem. This will explain why, an' I hope you understand." He moved to his wagon and gently called, "Sonja, come here, honey."

A young girl, eight or nine years old, poked her head through a slit in the flap at the rear of their wagon. "What you want, Papa?"

Blackwood tipped his hat. "Good afternoon, miss." Then he met the eyes of the gray-haired man. "I understand," he said, and moved to mount up. It was their camp and their right to refuse them entry.

The young men started to put up a clatter, and one said, "Aw, Pa, don't think it would hurt none for them to just stop an' rest."

"Hold on a minute, stranger," the father said. "I got to admit, sometimes I am a little quick." He studied on it a moment, giving Blackwood the once-over, then seemed to see what he was looking for, and said, "Naw, don't guess it would hurt none for you to rest here a spell."

"I'll make sure the girls mind their ways." Blackwood didn't feel insulted by the father taking his time to come to a decision. Letting a young girl mingle with whores was something for anyone to think twice about.

"Then you are welcome." He thrust his hand out as if he knew Blackwood was a man of his word, and said, "I'm Klas Ericsson, that one over there is my oldest, John, this is the youngest, Tate, an' that's Jim an' Tad. You met Sonja, here."

Blackwood shook hands all around and told

them his name. The boys, each in turn, welcomed him to the camp.

"That's a likely spot to pull a wagon, Mr. Blackwood." Klas Ericsson gestured to an area under a tree not too near his wagon.

Blackwood stepped to his horse, pulled himself into the saddle, and sent the piebald into a slow walk toward the girls.

"There's five men an' a small girl in their camp," he said, drawing up to the wagon. "They say we are welcome as long as you keep in mind the young girl." His eyes traveled over them and saw they were in stages of undress. "I suggest all of you put on some clothes. And keep them on. I gave my word there wouldn't be any getting out of line, an' I expect you to help me keep it." His voice bore a sharp edge.

"What?" Maybel sputtered as she hastily pulled a dress over her head and commenced to poke at her hair.

Francine bristled; putting one hand on her hip she held the other out, straight as an arrow, and pointed at him. "I'll have you know, *Mis*ter Blackwood, we know how to behave. After all, we are from the Pink Palace, the finest house in New Orleans. We are perfect ladies, an' quite civilized. I also want you to know, when we entertained gentlemen in the parlor, with our singing and conversation, it was in full attire. We did not drag men off the street and flop on a cot." She lifted her chin with a haughty jerk.

"Besides, that's what we're doing, dressing. We saw you shaking hands."

Maybel, Lily, Cora, and Francine glared at him, while Jenny's face held a puzzled look, and Wilma said, with a scowl, "Don't look at me. I'd just as soon not meet them anyway."

Such a long speech from Francine struck Blackwood as funny. Till now she had not said more than ten words to him. He held back the smile beginning to curl his lips. "Didn't mean to get you all that riled up." He removed his hat, ran his fingers through his hair, giving himself time to overcome the laugh he felt coming on.

The Pink Palace meant nothing to him, he'd never been to New Orleans. But it was obvious they expected him to show respect.

"I owe all you ladies an apology. Yep, imagine I do. Please forgive my ignorance. I had no idea you came from that house." He didn't scoff but couldn't regard it in quite the manner they wanted him to. "And now, when you ladies are ready." He made a sweeping bow, as best he could on horseback. "Lily, please drive the team, and I'll show you where to put the wagon."

Lily guided the wagon under a tree, near a crystal-clear stream. It was a well-protected area; on one side was a high bluff with water spilling over it to form a pool at the bottom. Giant boulders lay about, tall pine trees huddled close on the foothills.

The girls piled out of the wagon, all talking at the same time, and sliding glances at the men.

The young men were elbowing each other, their bright eyes showing a great deal of interest, and their grins turning to broad smiles as Blackwood introduced them.

The boys moved off with Lily, Francine, and Cora, some unhitched the mules while others helped carry items from the wagon.

Klas Ericsson, his hand extended, walked to Maybel. "Welcome to the camp."

"Thank you, Mr. Ericsson." Maybel smiled, shaking his hand. "Ain't you the lucky one, four big strapping boys and this lovely lady." Maybel patted Sonja on the head.

"Oh my, she is pretty," Jenny agreed, as she came forward. "Hello, I am Jenny," she said to Sonja. "I bet I have something in the wagon you will like. Cora says it's called pray-lean candy. Do you like sweeting?" When Sonja shyly nodded, Jenny continued. "After I fix something to eat for everyone, I'll find it, but you must eat first." Jenny moved toward the wagon for the food needed to prepare the meal.

Maybel gave Mr. Ericsson a charming smile. "I do hope you haven't ate, an' will join us?"

"That's right nice of you, Miss Maybel. The boys gathered firewood but I've not started to cook as yet." He smiled back at her nervously. "If you will excuse me, I'll give the boys the good news that they won't have to eat my bad cooking."

The Ericsson boys had picketed the mules in good grass not far from their oxen, and were

hanging around the girls on the pretext of helping.

Klas Ericsson and Blackwood mounted their
horses to ride a wide circle around the camp.
Since Blackwood was not a talkative man and
Ericsson much the same, they scouted every
crest and hollow in near silence.

Ericsson cleared his throat, breaking the
quiet. "Why don't you plan on spending the
night, Mr. Blackwood? Can't be more than a
couple, three hours of light left. You're welcome
to stay if you want an' ain't in no hurry to get on
up the trail."

Chapter Eight

HAVING TURNED NORTH they were now a short
jaunt from camp.

"Folks don't hang a mister on the front of my
name, they just call me Blackwood, Mr. Ericsson. I'll talk to the girls first, but I figger it's best
we stay the night. Wouldn't get far before dark
anyway."

"I was thinking along the same lines. It'll be a
good change, to set by the campfire and swap
windies." Ericsson squinted at the sky then set
his gaze momentarily on Blackwood. "By the

way, I'd be obliged if you'd call me Klas." He said it as if he knew the measure of the man and would like to also call him friend.

His gentle but firm manner reminded Blackwood of his own father.

"Well, it looks like there's nothing out here but scenery." Klas broke in on Blackwood's thoughts. "We best get back. If the food is ready and those boys get to it there won't be much left." He laughed.

The sun was slipping toward the western horizon when they approached camp. Guiding their horses to a small sweet grass meadow a few yards from camp, they stepped to the ground as Maybel bore down on them. "Glad you're back. You been gone better part of an hour, an supper's near ready."

Blackwood lifted his head and sniffed. "Smells like it's going to be a feast."

"Uh-huh, sure does," Klas said, lifting his saddle, hiking it to his shoulder, and moving toward his wagon.

Maybel turned to follow.

"Maybel." Blackwood called her to him. "Don't suppose we made more than ten miles today, but might as well settle in for the night. Couldn't get far before sundown, anyway." He dropped his saddle and bedroll under a tree on a slight incline. Pulling a scrap of a towel from his saddlebag he headed to the stream.

"That's a good idea," she said, walking double

time to keep up with him. "We can have us a good time."

He stopped short and raised his brows. "What you plannin', Maybel?"

"Oh...You can't mean we have to worry who's out there and be quiet again tonight?"

"With the Ericsson's here, don't think that's something to fret about. I'm interested in what kinda whing-ding you got in mind."

"I'll have the boys help me move the pump organ out of the wagon, and we'll have a sing." She gave him a wily smile. "What did you think I meant?"

"Pump organ, you got one of those on that wagon?" he asked, ignoring her question.

"Well, it's small but that's what it is."

After supper, Klas and Blackwood sat on a fallen log, hunched close to the campfire, their hands wrapped around steaming cups of coffee.

"The women surprised me. What I mean is, they don't act...Well. They're not what a body would expect." Klas paused, took a swallow from his cup, and changed the subject.

"There's a bite in the air this evening." Raising his head he scanned the twilight heavens. "Looks like it's gonna be one of those pitch-dark nights."

Blackwood silently nodded. Taking out his tobacco and paper, he began to build himself a smoke.

His eyes raked the area, taking inventory. Maybel and Lily were enlisting the aid of Jim and Tad, motioning them to follow. Cora and Francine headed upstream through a small clump of scrub pine. Jenny and Tate were returning from the creek, his arms laden with clean pots and pans. John sauntered toward the campfire with Sonja skipping along in front of him.

"Sit, son." Klas patted the space beside him on the log.

"We're going to have some music, Paw," he said, taking a small dry limb away from his sister as she started to poke at the fire. "You know better. Stay back," he reprimanded her.

Blackwood's eyes swept the camp again looking for Wilma. He put his cup down, stood, stretched, intending to stir around to see if he could spot her. At that moment she came from behind the wagon with a bedroll in her arms, almost colliding with Tate, who was walking beside Jenny. Wilma started to step aside to let them pass, changed her mind, glared at Tate then whirled, going back in the direction she came from.

Klas slightly dipped his head in Wilma's direction. "Don't mix much, does she?"

"Nope, she's a hard one to figger," Blackwood conceded as he picked up the coffee pot, offering some to Klas before filling his own cup.

"What in tarnation is that?" Klas questioned, staring at the pump organ his sons were carrying toward them.

Maybel and Francine make music on it, or so

they say." John sounded skeptical as he stood to give them a hand.

"It's pretty level here. Sit it down. Careful," Maybel instructed. Placing a small round stool in front of the box, she lifted the lid to expose the keys and inquired, "Where's Francine?"

"She be right back," answered Jenny.

The men were milling about inspecting the odd-looking box as Maybel explained how it worked. "You press these and they make musical notes."

Klas pushed down on one of the keys; it made no sound. "I don't hear anything," he said.

She pointed to two slats near the base with straps leading up into the box. "First, you have to pump these with your feet." She sat on the stool, her feet on the slats pushing first one, then the other. Her fingers poised over the keyboard, she began to play.

Lifting her head she glanced at Klas. "Sing, Mr. Ericsson."

He backed away. "Not me, my voice is like a catamount howling in the wilds."

Maybel gave Blackwood a questioning look, "You?"

Blackwood held up his hands. "Not me, either. But if I remember right, when Francine gave her speech she said she could sing." He grinned roguishly.

"And I can." Francine stepped forward, opened her mouth, and a beautiful clear tone came forth.

The men were astonished. Not only did she have beauty, but also a brilliant singing voice.

Francine sang the song's last stanza:

> *"As I look back o'er the years*
> *I know I had my hours*
> *And I'll cry no tears*
> *Even tho' I'm now a faded flower."*

There was awed silence after the last clear note faded into the dark night. After the fleeting moment, they began milling around her shouting their approval.

Lily moved to stand next to Blackwood, and ground out in a low voice, "We do have to admit she can sing."

Blackwood raised his head; Francine's eyes met his square on. Her lips were curled in a smirk. He knew he owed her the acknowledgment and he mouthed, "Very good."

Maybel speedily pumped the pedals, and her fingers flew over the keys as she began to pound out a lively tune.

"Listen to this. Come on, girls, let's sing a New Orleans song for them." She shouted, "Here we go now!"

Cora's, Lily's, and Francine's voices joined Maybel's as they sang, and the best Blackwood could make out was, "Jump, jump up, jump, jump down." Lily grabbed Klas, and all but Blackwood were partnered. They were stomping and swinging their legs in time with the music. Blackwood sat on the log to watch. It was what

they needed to raise their spirits after all that
had happened this day.

Hearing a wild cry from the ridge above camp
Blackwood tuned out the camp noise to listen.
Unless you had the edge of knowing the difference, it was impossible to tell a true animal call
from an Indian signal.

Chapter Nine

WHEN THE OUTCRY split the air again, Blackwood knew it was the call of an animal.

Klas tired out and turned his partner over to
John. Collecting Sonja, he joined Blackwood.
"Whew! That will stove-up an old man, fast." He
settled himself on the log.

"Looked to me you were doing pretty good."
Blackwood's eyes were on the gyrations of the
dancers. "Sometimes it's good to exert yourself
a little extra. It helps work a bad day out of your
system."

Klas threw Blackwood a puzzled look. "Didn't
happen across two scruffy, mean-eyed vermin
today, did yuh?" he asked.

"Yeah, we did."

"Thought I recognized that sorrel tied to the
back of your wagon."

Blackwood told him of the murdered family he found and the two that had admitted the killing. He wound the story up, saying, "They got pretty rough with the girls before I was able to get back to them."

Klas nodded. "I understand. They started a scrap with me, long about first light. When my boys rode up the odds weren't to their liking, and they hightailed it out of sight."

Blackwood's thoughts jumped to what slowpokes the Ericssons were to have traveled such a short distance since early morning.

As if to read his silence, Klas said, "That wagon is awkward an' heavy. It's not built for speed. We're only making about ten miles a day."

"You're not in a hurry to get where you're going?" Blackwood questioned.

"Sure, but not so's I want to lose anything on that wagon. My brother and I prepared for this move for over a year, an' we can't afford any mistakes. We're traveling slow an' cautious. Building strength for when we need it an' leaving nothing to chance. My brother an' his family are waiting in Oregon for a couple of those critters"—he motioned toward the oxen—"and part of that equipment. He went on ahead 'bout nine, ten months ago to buy land."

Klas's gaze had been fixed for several minutes. Blackwood followed his stare and saw Tate and Jenny had dropped away from the dancing. They were lolling against a tree, talking and laughing. To one side in the shadows, near the wagon, Wilma was watching them.

Klas glanced at Blackwood. "Don't want no trouble."

Blackwood took him to mean he was apprehensive about Wilma staring at Jenny and Tate. "Shouldn't be none. Wilma just looks out for Jenny."

With a hint of curiosity in his voice Klas mumbled, "I wonder why?"

Blackwood shrugged. "I reason it's 'cause she got her this job of cooking an' cleaning."

"That's all Jenny does? Cook an' clean?" He eyed Blackwood with narrowed interest.

"Yep, that's it." Blackwood nodded.

"Hum," Klas murmured. His eyes turned bright and a secret smile hovered about his mouth. "I was hoping one of my boys would get bitten an' take a fancy to someone. Didn't think it might be Tate." He chuckled before continuing. "Him being the youngest, an' too durn hard to please. Never known him to corner a gal before." The smile slowly slipped from his face and a pensive expression took over. "I knew right off my Beth was right for me an' we married three days later. Had a good life together, too. She took sick soon after Sonja was born, an' was gone in no time." Blackwood heard him catch his breath. "I sorely miss that woman."

Sonja tugged at her father's sleeve. "What's fancy, Papa? Did Tate get bitten?"

"Hey! It's time you were in bed." Klas picked

her up and swung her around. "Be right back, soon's this little lady is tucked in."

A frown creased Blackwood's brow as he observed Wilma still staring at Jenny and Tate. It seemed odd. But even if it was strange, it caused no harm, and finally dismissing it, he began to listen to the song Maybel was singing.

When Klas returned he stood a moment studying the area. As his gaze fell on Wilma he said thoughtfully, "She hasn't moved." He slowly shook his head in a bewildered motion. "It's not my business an' you can tell me to hush, if you want. I been noticin' the looks that gal shoots you, an' it's clear you're not one of her favorite people. I know—her being a gal an' all—but wouldn't hurt none if a fella was to keep his eyes open." Perching on the log again, the pitch of his voice changed as he said, "Wonder if there's anything in that pot?" Picking up the tin cup he had used earlier, he filled it with the steaming, strong brew.

Blackwood slid him a knowing look. "Staying alert is what keeps me alive."

Klas nodded somberly and lifted his cup almost to his lips. "Suppose we should call a halt to all this folderol? Won't be a one of them wanting to get up come morning...an'...." Hesitatingly his voice faded as if a new thought came to him. He took a cautious sip of the hot coffee and spoke fast, as if he wanted to get it said before he changed his mind. "What say we travel together a day or two? Accordin' to my calculations me an' the boys have about that much travelin' time, in this direction, before we have to angle south." When Blackwood opened his mouth to object, Klas quickly continued. "Now don't hesitate to say we're going too slow for you. I just had some crazy idea about Tate an' Jenny," he confessed, looking guilty.

With his eyes cast on the toe of his boots, Blackwood grumbled to himself. I started this trek believing it would take a couple weeks or so. Sandy's trail will be colder than a well digger's ass by the time I get to the Boise Basin. But damn-it-all-to-hell, Jenny does deserve a chance and it's bound to be a better life than she has now. Anyway, what's two days? He argued with himself a few moments longer, then shifting his gaze to Klas, said out loud, "Sounds all right to me. Maybe something good will come from it. What will be, will be." He didn't entirely mean for Jenny's sake, he also meant in his search.

Blackwood and Klas sauntered toward Maybel, halting in front of her as she finished her song. "'Bout time to call it a night, ain't it?" Blackwood asked, but it sounded more like an order.

The young folks were in high spirits and did not want to bring the evening to an end. They bombarded Blackwood and Klas with grumbles and sour looks.

Klas's eyes darted to Blackwood. "It seems they think we are depriving them of a good time."

"Let them tell themselves that in the morning," Blackwood suggested.

While Klas instructed two of his sons to replace the organ in the wagon, Blackwood gestured to Maybel. "Come, have a seat by the fire." He poked at the campfire, replenishing it with a large log before settling down beside her. "We are gonna travel with the Ericsson party," he bluntly stated. "That means it will take longer, maybe a day or therebouts, before we reach those mines you...ah..."—his voice faltered—wanted to...ah...visit."

Maybel turned sharply from him. "You can't do this to us. We need every cent we can get from those miners. We need lots of money. When we get to San Francisco, we want to open a real nice place. It just won't happen if we don't... entertain on the way there." She looked dejected, then seemed to brighten as she asked, "Could we...you know...sort of secret like... with the Ericssons? I'm sure they're interested." She turned to face him expectantly. "Then the delay wouldn't be a total loss." She ended by giving him a pouty look.

"I gave my word, Maybel, unless Klas changes his mind, I intend to keep it and see that you do, too." He stood looking down at her.

"Ah can see your mind is made up. I don't like it, but all right. I surely hope we're not held up more than two days." She rose facing him and he saw a look in her eyes he did not quite trust.

Chapter Ten

EVERYONE WAS BEDDED down by the time Blackwood turned in. He was troubled; an uneasy feeling kept him from falling asleep. Going over the evening's events he tried to come up with what was agitating him. Jenny and Tate had lingered after everyone was settled in, but not long enough for it to be disturbing, he dismissed it. Again he went over all that had occurred and it came to him. Maybel had taken an uncommon amount of time bidding Klas good night. He could see her in his mind's eye, all smiles and gestures. Her actions reminded him of their first encounter, when she had tried to sweet-talk him out of noticing the gold shortage when he was hired for this job.

"Damn," he grumbled softly to himself, "I even gave her a clue by saying she couldn't ply her trade unless Klas changed his mind. By damn, I bet she's gonna try to get him to alter his decision."

A cool breeze brushed across him as he lay with his arms folded behind his head. A small smile began to play about his mouth as he stared at the clear, star-speckled sky. "That little gal is a clever one, an' just might pull it off. What the hell, they're all big boys," he told himself and rolled over on his side.

He had again spread his bedroll in a spot giving a clear view of the wagons, and he now lay with his eyes pinned in their direction. Hearing a faint thump and scrape, he saw feet then legs snake out the back of the girls' wagon. The flickering campfire played across Maybel's face as she gave herself a boost off the tail end. Landing quietly, she gathered up her skirts and quickly vanished into the brush.

Blackwood kept vigil. He judged she was gone the better part of an hour when he heard the rustle of her return.

The noise caused Jenny and Lily to stir. Wilma woke, crawled from under the prairie schooner, and confronted Maybel. "Where have you been?" Her voice raised in an angry hiss carried to Blackwood.

Maybel threw her chin up in defiance. "Ah have been known to get up a time or two in the middle of the night," she hissed back. Then quickly putting her finger across her lips said, "Shush, you want to wake everyone? Hush up an' get back to bed," she curtly ordered, and climbed into the back of the wagon, leaving Wilma standing alone.

A smile curled Blackwood's lips. He knew why Maybel was ill-tempered. Klas had not kept the appointment she tried to set up.

The wagons were roughly a mile behind when Blackwood and John Ericsson rounded the rise on tired horses. They had been in the saddle and blazing trail since the first streak of light signaled dawn. They pulled their mounts up to survey the area, looking for a suitable place to pause for the noon meal.

Below, a short distance to the north, was a towering rock wall. A large boulder jutted from this escarpment, forming a wide shelf high enough to pull the girls' wagon under with room to spare. Nearby was an outfall, small but adequate.

A brisk wind was pushing the white clouds from the blue skies, and dark thunderheads peeked over the mountaintops.

"Looks like we might be in for a little weather." John raised his head, scanning the sky.

Blackwood fastened his eyes on the ominous dark clouds, slowly following their course. "We're in luck, most of it is north of us an' moving east."

A crack of lightning flashed across the peaks to touch somewhere in the valley beyond. In the distance could be heard a rumble rolling about the heavens.

The piebald did a frog step, shook its head, and snorted. "But no doubt we are in for some rain," Blackwood conceded, stroking his pony on the neck.

"That looks like a good place to hole up till it's over." John gestured toward the towering rock spied earlier.

"Let's have a look-see." Blackwood nudged his horse forward.

"Looks like a popular spot," he said, pointing to several burned-out campfires scattered about. Dismounting he checked the ashes. "They're mighty cold. Been awhile since this place had tenants." He kicked at the cold ashes while his eyes traveled up the black smoke deposits left on the rocks by the past campfires. "A few wore paint and feathers," he said, hunkering down to examine the ground. "But, been awhile." He held up a broken arrowhead. "How's about you gathering firewood while I ride out an' bring in the wagons?" Blackwood jerked his head in the direction of the rest of the party. "Well, reckon we ought to be gettin' to it, so's we can beat the rain." He slowly rose and moved toward his pony.

"Sounds good to me," John said, then added, "That's a good horse. Ain't you afraid he'll take off on you, leaving him loose like that?"

"Nope, he's Indian-trained. As long as that rein touches the ground, he'll stand till hell freezes over," he drawled, then mounted up and took out toward the wagons.

"Pull her in about there—just a mite more to the right—that's good," Blackwood shouted as Lily guided the wagon in close to the back wall, set the brake, and jumped down to unharness the mules.

Klas pulled in behind her, his wagon a little more than half under the shelter. His boys quickly unhitched the oxen and were leading them to grass when Klas called out, "How 'bout a couple of you boys taking care of these mules for this little lady." He walked up to Lily. "That's a mighty fine piece of work. You handle them mules pretty slick."

Lily gave him an uncertain titter. "Thank ya, Mr. Ericsson. Been praised for lots of things but this is a sho'-nuf first for my mule-skinning." The look on her face said that she received mighty few flattering remarks that didn't require her flat on her back.

Blackwood was picketing his horse as the deluge hit. When he dashed back under the shelter he was dripping wet. "Those raindrops are so big, each one would water a good-sized field," he exaggerated with a grin and moved to the fire to dry off.

Suddenly, the shelter was lit by a bright zigzag flash, followed by an earsplitting snap, and a reverberating rumble tumbled about overhead.

Jenny jumped, dropped a pan, gave a shriek as she brushed past Wilma and ran to Tate, burying her face in his chest.

Blackwood said, "That was close. Better check the stock."

As the odor of fervid heat reached them, the men ran to check the livestock.

"It hit on this side." Lily called them back. "See up there." She pointed to the next hill, which displayed a smoldering area where several trees were down.

"Lucky those animals were on the other side."
Klas wagged his head sidewise. "An' protected
by this mountain."

Some of the gloom disappeared as the campfire caught and began to burn bright and cheerful.

Tate, holding Jenny in the crook of his arm,
looked down at her and said, "It's awright now,
come on, I'll help you."

Klas glanced at Tate and Jenny and gave
Blackwood an "I-told-you-so" look, then raised
his brows at a loud slam, bang coming from the
girls' wagon.

Blackwood quickly scanned the camp and
saw that Wilma was not among them.

Maybel climbed into the wagon, they heard a
scuffle, then Maybel's voice with a sharp edge to
it snapped, "Stop it." then the voice's continued
in indistinguishable whispers.

When Maybel appeared at the portal, Wilma's
voice shrieked, "Y'all can just bring my food in
here. I'm not eating with those sod-busters."

As Klas helped Maybel to the ground, she
gave him a weak smile. "The storm has upset
her." She was visibly struggling with the embar-
rassment of knowing everyone had heard
Wilma.

Blackwood was fed up with Wilma's antics.
"Wet buffalo chips," he muttered softly. "Bet this
storm's afraid of her."

The dark rain clouds hung low, making the
day seem like twilight as everyone settled down

to the normal routine. The girls were busy fussing with the meal. Blackwood and Klas sat cross-legged near the fire. Klas tamped tobacco in his pipe while Blackwood took out his damp makings and built a smoke.

"Rain should be gone soon," Klas predicted.

"Yup." Blackwood nodded.

Jenny handed Klas a cup of coffee and was holding one out to Blackwood when he raised his hand for quiet.

"You hear something?" whispered Klas.

Blackwood nodded, uncrossed his legs, and stood.

Chapter Eleven

THE ERICSSON BOYS lifted their rifles, herded the girls to the rear, and formed a line in front of them. They stood easy with their rifles over their arms.

"There's two of them," Blackwood said as he pushed his holster down solid on his hips. Easing off the thong he lifted the pistol, then released it to slip back in place. He was satisfied with the ease it slid from the holster.

From beyond the line of trees a voice called out, "Two riders coming in."

Blackwood bid them enter.

Two men in yellow slickers with their hats low over their faces slowly materialized from behind the screen of trees. His saddle creaked as the one in front leaned forward. "Howdy, Blackwood," he said. "You still around? I heard someone took a dislike to you up around Sand Point and rid the world of your likes."

Recognizing the voice Blackwood said, "Well ... Stace Dillano, you heard wrong. Had me a bad time for awhile there, but I'm in good shape now." He eased off. "You and yore partner step down. I think we can spare a cup of coffee." Blackwood turned to Klas. "It's awright. I know this ol' boy."

When they stepped into camp Stace motioned toward his partner. "Blackwood, this is my brother Clayton. Don't think you ever met him."

Blackwood nodded at Clayton, saying, "Shuck your slickers and set a spell."

They removed the rain gear and hung them over the tongue of Klas's wagon. They were dressed as ordinary cowboys, from their scuffed, run-down boots to their crushed wide-brim hats. They appeared to be of the same caliber as Blackwood, but harder and older. The conspicuous difference was they both wore silver stars on the left side of their vests.

Blackwood introduced the marshal and his deputy to the girls, then to Klas said, "Stace and Clayton Dillano are out of the silver city in the

Washoe region." Klas shook hands and in turn introduced his sons.

The girls melted into the background, with the exception of Jenny. Jenny rushed forward with coffee.

After the men were settled on the hard ground, Blackwood asked, "Well, Stace, what brings you this far out of your territory?"

Stace exhaled a puff of smoke. "Aw, a ways north of here they're holding two prisoners. We aim to take them back." He shrugged his shoulders nonchalantly. "Pressure put on by a money man back home. I think he's dumb enough to believe they'll still have some of the bank money on 'em," he said sourly, then snorted, "Ain't that a laugh? They probably spent all that money plus someone else's on whoring an' gambling by now." He spoke softly for Blackwood's and Klas's ears alone. "A sheriff up around Hot Springs caught 'em rustlin' beeves. He should have gone ahead an' hung them. Maybe he has an' this'll be a wasted trip." The look on his face said that would really get his dander up, after he came all this way then end up going back empty-handed.

"Aw, Stace, you're just getting crotchety." Clayton poked fun at his brother.

Blackwood glanced at Stace. "Gettin'? He's been that way ever since I've known him."

"You two"—Klas waved his hand at Stace and Blackwood—"go back a ways, huh?"

"Sure do," Stace answered then squinted at

Blackwood. "You taken to being a wagonmaster or just riding with this party?" He cocked his head forward, waiting for his reply.

"You're half right." Blackwood shifted his position. "Came across these ladies, they needed a pinch of help to get to Fort Boise." He paused, turned to Klas. "Now you take Klas Ericsson here. He don't need help, as you can readily tell by just lookin'. Him an his boys're doing fine. We're enjoying each other's company for a couple days, while traveling in the same direction."

"Where you bound, Ericsson?" Stace asked.

"Nosy, ain't he? Been a lawman so long it's a habit with him," Blackwood interjected.

"That's all right." Klas dismissed his prying. "We are on our way to a place in the Oregon Territory called the Willamette Valley. That's north of the Klamath Lakes an' a mite beyond the Umpqua region. We have family and some good fertile land waiting for us there."

"Well, lots of luck, and like Blackwood sez you'll do just fine." Stace glanced at the Ericsson boys standing easy but still holding their rifles. Walking from under the overhang he peered at the blue sky that was still holding a few patchy clouds. "Mount up, Clayton, rain's over, and we gotta move out." Placing his hands on his hips he bent backward to stretch out the kinks.

"Ain't you staying to have a bite to eat with us?" Jenny questioned. "It's ready an' we'd be happy to have you."

"She's a mighty fine cook." Tate laid his hand on Jenny's shoulder. "An' you'll miss a good meal if you don't stay."

Stace's lips cracked in a smile, as if they were not accustomed to the activity. "I don't doubt she is a good cook. But we have quite a piece to travel and it's best we get moving." Being a Westerner he was a perfect gentleman when speaking to or about a decent woman. "I know your wife makes good coffee." He lifted his cup, swallowed the last mouthful, and handed the empty cup to Jenny.

Blackwood chuckled to himself; in the confusion of introducing everyone, Stace must have assumed Jenny was with the Ericsson party.

Jenny's face flushed as she dropped her eyes and softly said, "We ain't married."

Flustered, Stace blurted out, "Oh! I thought sure you were...I mean you should be...I mean—" He clamped his mouth shut, laying bare, if he said more he would only compound the blunder.

From experience, Blackwood knew Stace could take a joshing. "What's the matter, Stace? You look like you have more in your mouth than your throat will swallow." His thoughts raced to the times Stace had poked a few jibes at him. He wasn't about to miss this opportunity for a turnabout.

Clayton's eyes were bright, he was warming up to make a few taunting remarks of his own.

"Yeah," he exclaimed. "What's the matter, big brother?"

"Stop the fooling, Clayton, an' mount up, we gotta get," Stace lashed out, while his eyes told Blackwood to go ahead and laugh, ol' Stace would have his turn another day.

It was obvious to everyone Stace was in for a hard time from his brother.

Jenny glanced from Stace to Clayton. "Hold on a minute," she said. After a moment she returned and handed Stace a cloth bundle. "It's something for you and your brother to eat. If you want to share with him."

Stace as well as everyone caught her meaning. If Clayton plagued him on the trail he could threaten to eat all the food himself.

"Thank you," Stace said simply and dipped his head.

They turned their mounts. Raising a hand in farewell, they rode out of camp, with Clayton looking subdued.

"That was thoughtful of you, Jenny." Tate smiled at her.

"She sure saved his bacon," laughed Blackwood.

"And I bet his brother wasn't even primed yet." Klas joined Blackwood in laughing at the predicament Stace had gotten himself entangled in.

"You shouldn't make fun of a person's mistakes," Jenny reprimanded. But anyone could tell Blackwood would do it again if the occasion arose.

As Jenny began to dish up, the other girls joined them, making themselves comfortable around the fire. Even Wilma came out of the wagon to sit beside Maybel.

"I'm glad the rain stopped"—Maybel stared at the sky—"maybe we can make a few more miles before sundown." She then turned to Blackwood with a questioning look. "Were those friends of yours? What did they want?"

Didn't want nothing"—Blackwood scrutinized her—"only a rest out of the rain."

"But what did they say?" she persisted.

"Not a helluva lot. Why?" he answered in an offhand manner.

Maybel's face took on a blank look. "I was only wondering what y'all were whispering about." When he didn't readily answer, her tone of voice and expression changed. "Must be a secret...."

Blackwood frowned at her. "You sure got a burr under your tail."

"Just forget it," she snapped.

He studied her. "Weren't any secrets, mostly talk about the prisoners they were going after. The rest was tongue wagglin'." He shrugged. But his mind was working on the reasons she might be disturbed about a conversation. Also, why had Wilma changed her mind about eating with them? Had Wilma prompted Maybel to question him?

Chapter Twelve

ON A HUNCH Blackwood leaned forward, fixed his gaze on Wilma, and asked, "Anything else you want to know?"

The look on her face as she scooted behind Maybel told him his hunch was right. He stood. "If not, I suggest we rouse ourselves an' make tracks. Agreeable with you, Klas?"

"Good idea," Klas answered as he rose, saying to his sons, "Awright, boys, time to clear camp. An'...uh...you...Jim, let Sonja ride with you for awhile. I want to have a word with Blackwood." Klas's shadow fell across Blackwood as he moved to walk beside him. "How 'bout Tate an' John taking point an' you ridin' with me for a spell, so we can talk?"

Blackwood nodded as they continued to move toward the narrow stream. They scooped up small pebbles and sand from the creek bottom, ground it around on their dirty dishes, then rinsed them in the clear water.

With a burst of energetic action they were ready to move out in less than thirty minutes. Lily snapped the whip over the mules' heads and they stepped out in perfect unison. Klas's oxen were much slower, giving Blackwood time to tie the piebald to the rear of the wagon and swing aboard. After a bit of polite palaver the talk died and the squeak of the wheels or the slap of the ribbons was the only noise to break the silence.

Blackwood waited, knowing as soon as Klas worked out how to say what he had on his mind he would speak up. Finally Klas cleared his throat and spoke. "I'll speak plain, if'n you don't mind?"

"That's the best way," advised Blackwood.

Klas slid him a sideways glance. "Them gals are losing out on some money traveling this slow, wouldn't you say?"

"Maybel has been at you, hasn't she?" Blackwood asked, then firmly stated, "Well, you don't have to worry 'cause I gave my word."

"I ain't complaining about Maybel. No, one of the other gals mentioned the matter to John." He peered at Blackwood from under the brim of his hat. "What I do have on my hands is three healthy boys with an itch in their crotches that only a gal can scratch. An' lord, are they hounding me something awful. Tate is pretty disgusted with his brothers, but he only has eyes for Jenny. Those other three are 'bout to become deranged." He snickered, cleared his throat again, and wiped the smile off his face. "Anyway, what I wanted was to release you from your word." He took a long breath and added, "That's if you are of a mind to?"

"Just one question. What about Sonja? She was the reason the rule was made." Blackwood hesitated, then continued, "No doubt you have that all worked out but I have to ask anyway."

"Everything is to be regular until Sonja is asleep and nothing—an' I mean nothing—is to go on inside the camp boundary."

Blackwood took a moment. It was all he could do to keep from laughing out loud. So, Maybel, you won. But I believed you would from the onset, because there is no accounting when it comes to man and woman. They won't rest until they can get together. Out loud he drawled, "I can't say I blame them boys, those gals are damn good-lookers." And persistent, he added to himself, gave a silent sigh and unsaddled the responsibility from across his shoulders.

"I have to be honest, Blackwood. Every time Maybel swishes that behind in front of me I want to reach out and grab a handful." Klas let loose a boom of laughter.

"I know what you mean," chuckled Blackwood.

Klas turned serious. "They are good boys even if they don't always think clear. But they better follow my orders where Sonja is concerned, or I'll take the hide right off them."

Blackwood was confident Klas meant what he said. But by the evidence of these last couple days, he didn't think it would come to be a problem. The boys were like their father in many ways.

"I'll tell Maybel. Don't think it's necessary but I will caution her to use good judgment," Blackwood said.

"Thanks." Klas gave him a lopsided grin, then

put his foot on the brake while pulling back on the reins to halt the wagon. "I'll let the boys know. It'll sure make three lustful men happy," cackled Klas.

Blackwood hopped down from the wagon, untied his horse, and mounted up. Passing the wagon at a lope he raised his hand in a salute. "I'll send one of the boys back from point." His pony shot forward in an all-out run, as if grateful for the exercise after the slow walk.

Drawing up beside the girls' wagon he said angrily, "Lily, you keep up this pace and you'll be too far ahead of the Ericsson wagon. Look back there, they're 'bout out of sight. You're gonna have to slow them mules down."

"They's goin' about as slow as they can now. Ain't my fault their wagon can't keep up," she pouted.

"Well, you'll have to slow them down some more. That's too big a gap," he stated tersely then asked, "Where's Maybel?"

Maybel stuck her head out the opening. "I'm here. What y'all want?"

"Lily, stop the wagon." His voice was flinty because she had not heeded his request to drop back.

When Lily pulled up he turned to Maybel. "I have something to tell you." He dismounted. "Here, let me help you down." Reaching up he clasped her around the waist and swung her to the ground. "Let's walk. It won't hurt none for the wagon to set a spell, you're too far ahead anyway."

When they moved a few feet from the wagon he told her what he and Klas had discussed. She let out a war whoop, threw her arms around him, and gave him a long, wanton kiss. She broke off long before he was ready to call it quits, and started thanking him.

"Weren't my idea," he said. "Klas came up with it."

"Anyway, I'm glad. I have to tell the girls." She gave Blackwood a big-eyed look. "Find us a good camp for tonight." Turning she ran back to the wagon.

Blackwood mounted up again. "Tate wouldn't be interested in the new development," he surmised, "so, John, you're the one I'll send back from point."

At the touch of Blackwood's heels the piebald stepped into a brisk trot. Blackwood's green eyes lightened as he hummed a little ditty: "There'll be a hot time in camp this night."

Chapter Thirteen

BLACKWOOD AND TATE wore wide-brimmed hats
pulled low to keep the blazing sun's glare out of
their eyes. Since the noon break they had traveled in a southwestern direction away from the
foothills. Most of the terrain hugging the mountains, to the north, had been too hazardous for
the wagons to cross.

Blackwood was aware that for some time
water had seemed to be getting scarce and he
grew concerned. "We best start looking for a
water hole or we'll be forced to make a dry
camp tonight. If we see only a trickle, we'll follow it north for a stretch, an' hope it will turn
large enough to at least water the stock."

Tate's smile was thin. "I'm in hopes we find
something soon. I'm hot, tired, an' hungry, ain't
you?" Removing his hat he rubbed the sweat off
his brow onto his shirtsleeve.

Blackwood did not answer because it seemed
he himself was always hot, tired, and hungry,
or cold, tired, and hungry. That had been a way
of life for him for quite a spell. The young man
sitting hunched in the saddle beside him did
appear to be worn out and could use a word of
encouragement. "I'd say ya still got a lot in
you, so don't give up yet." Observing that the
sun was edging close to the horizon, and in
two hours it would be twilight, Blackwood

added, "It'll be 'bout an hour before we stop."

"I was kinda banking on a pretty place to camp tonight." Tate shifted uncomfortably in the saddle. "I'm gonna ask Jenny to go with me, when we separate tomorrow." His voice held a note of concern as he squinted at Blackwood to see his reaction.

The expression on Blackwood's face was a careful look that did not betray how he felt. So with an air of self-confidence Tate continued. "The first preacher we come across, I want us to get married." With nothing left to say on the subject they nudged their horses forward.

As they topped the next hillock, three narrow streams came into view. The largest dribbled its way due south, the other two, threadlike, traveled along each side several feet apart.

"Would you take a gander at that. Luck is still riding beside us." Relief crossed Tate's face.

"It has possibilities. Spread out, we don't wanna make too good a target of ourselves," Blackwood said, for he knew you could never take anything for granted. Just when you thought there wasn't anyone for miles, hostiles could pop over the crest of a hill and in the bat of an eye you could be fighting for your life. "Head out that way." He gestured toward the north. "That appears to be a clump of trees a hoot-an'-holler up yonder. Let's have us a look-see." He nudged his horse forward, down the slight incline.

"Pretty level an' wide along that bank; won't

be much trouble getting the wagons in or out."
Tate twisted about looking the area over.

"Let's keep heading toward those trees. Keep
your eyes peeled an' your firearm handy. Never
forget we are edging close to Paiute country.
Been fairly peaceable for a long time along this
trail, but you never know." Blackwood studied
the surroundings. Where there was water there
were often others, and they were not always
friendly.

They headed upstream, a modest climb toward the stand of trees. As they rode past where
the creek divided they saw the width had spread
to fifteen feet or so, but looked to be only somewhere between eight or ten inches deep. They
felt the coolness of the shade as the area opened
into a wide, flat glade with a few large boulders
nearby. The trees with their bright green spring
leaves formed canopies over much of the area.

"This the kinda spot ya had in mind for tonight?" Blackwood smiled as Tate gazed in awe
at the beauty surrounding them. "Let's circle to
see if we have neighbors."

They rode across the creek and circled back,
recrossing the stream. Having seen nothing but
small wild game on either side, Tate elected to
dismount.

"If you want to gather fuel for a fire"—Blackwood gestured toward the dead tree limbs lying
about—"I'll ride to bring in the wagons."

"Fair enough, an' maybe I can trap a couple
of those birds we saw. Be good for supper.

Who'eee, I can't wait to eat." Tate was already removing his saddle and hobbling his horse.

Pivoting the piebald, Blackwood grinned. The young always seem to be hungry.

Just as Tate had predicted it was easy going for the wagons up the slope to the clearing.

When the girls' wagon pulled in, Tate helped unhitch the mules and rushed to picket them in a nearby grassy meadow. Quickly returning he raised his arms to help Jenny to the ground.

"You needn't bother. I can help myself." White-lipped she brushed his hands aside.

"Suit yourself." He stepped back, studying her. She looked changed. Her usual cheerful face was drawn and her jaw hard-set.

"If you hand me some of the supplies you'll need, I'll carry them for you." He tried again.

She turned on him. "I haven't the slightest intention of letting you do anything for me. If you will remove yourself, I will tend to everything. Get out of my way!" Sparks flew from her bright blue eyes.

Tate shrank from the wrath in her tone. "What put you on the prod? The stock needs tending now, but we'll talk later." As he moved toward the meadow he muttered to himself, "By the time I finish, I hope she's got a handle on whatever is eatin' her."

Tate ignored the warm sun of the late April day and the new grass pushing up from the rich earth that only recently had shed its white winter coat. He frowned as he helped his brothers move the mules and oxen to water and grass in a safe meadow not too far from camp.

Meanwhile, back at the campsite, Maybel, Francine, Lily, and Cora were in high spirits and looked as if they had spent most of the afternoon in front of a mirror. They were visions in radiant silk dresses with scraps of ribbons or plumes tucked in their twisted and coiled hair.

The girls lined up beside Maybel, as if on display, and a low murmur commenced to ripple as the men ogled them.

Maybel raised her hand for attention and in her throaty Southern drawl announced, "As this is our last supper together we planned a celebration. Instead of the usual fare, Jenny and all of us"—she indicated the girls with a sweep of her hand—"will fix a meal like y'all could only get at the finest dining room in New Orleans." She paused, giving Blackwood and the Ericssons a bright smile. "Well—maybe not quite that good. Now, this is the bill of fare, so you can set your mouths for something good and not grumble 'cause it's taking a long time to fix." All eyes remained on Maybel. "First off, thanks to Tate we'll have some of those birds he caught nearby. Next, a stew with corn dumplings, an' I think we got some okra that ain't spoiled. Also fried wild onions with side meat and what we call back home Washday Special—that's beans with rice. Ah guess that's about it." She looked thoughtful for a moment then quickly added, "Oh, one other thing. Lily's gonna make some shortbread." She then set the girls to their chores.

As Francine moved off to contribute her share, she stopped suddenly. With a flutter of her hand she drew their attention. Striking a seductive pose, she cast her eyes over her shoulder and said, "I really hope y'all don't think the whole evening's delights is just filling the empty space in your stomachs." She flashed the men an enticing smile that never quite reached her eyes.

Chapter Fourteen

THE GIRLS' HUMMING and singing could be heard over the crackle of the fire and the banging of pots as they went about their work. Jenny's face displayed a frown with lips drawn thin and tight. While perched on a large fallen log the Ericssons tossed needling remarks and playful punches at each other. Their eyes strayed now and again to the girls on the other side of the campfire. Sonja, being so young, was ignorant of what caused their cheerfulness, but picking up on their good mood she danced about happily.

While observing the gleam in the Ericsson boys' eyes, Blackwood recollected, It's been a long time since I've dipped my wick. Almost made it the other night with Maybel...if that damn fight hadn't broke out. He shrugged mentally. What the hell, let the Ericssons pay for it, if they want, damned if I will. The only pleasures I'll pay for are a bottle of whiskey or trying my luck at a game of faro.

The lighthearted atmosphere gave Tate confidence as he returned to camp and stepped close to Jenny. "I'd offer my help but looks like you have plenty." He motioned toward the other girls.

Her lips tight, Jenny threw him a dark look, and wrapped her hand around the handle of a pan. "If you don't get away an' stay away from me, I'm gonna let you have it with this."

"All right." He held up his hands in surrender, stepped backward then moved to the other side of the fire, and dropped down beside Blackwood. With an elbow braced against his knee he leaned on his hand for a time, to watch her.

"What's the matter, Tate? You look like someone licked all the red off your candy," teased John, letting loose a peal of laughter. Tad, Jim, and their father joined in.

Tate rolled his head to the side, glaring at them. "I'd be happy if all of you would mind your own business. Dad, you surprise me."

"Why? Your mother always did say you boys got all the devil in you from me."

Blackwood's mind was occupied with speculating about the evening's events when Jenny roughly thrust a cup of coffee at him and some of the hot liquid sloshed on his hand. "Damn!" he cussed, quickly transferring the cup to the other hand, and began to fan the burned hand back and forth to ease the stinging. "What the hell's the matter with you?" But he was talking to the back of her head as she moved away faster than she had approached.

"You're lucky. I got almost the whole cup spilled on me." Tate was fanning the leg of his trousers to take the heat out. "She's in a temper for some reason I can't figger." His face was shadowed with a troubled expression.

Blackwood glanced at the other men. They were sitting relaxed, sipping their coffee; she hadn't scalded them. "What goes on here? Why's she after our hides? What did you say to her, Tate?" Blackwood frowned.

"Nothin' at all. When their wagon rolled in I went to help her. She said she didn't need me. Then I tried talkin' to her again, over by the campfire. She said she'd clobber me with a fry pan if I didn't stay away from her."

With a questioning look Blackwood said, "Everybody's in a good mood. Wonder what riled her?"

Tate tugged at his pants again, glared at his father, and said, "You think it's funny, Dad?"

Klas nodded.

Abruptly it struck Blackwood. "Damn, I'm a featherhead. I know what's the matter with her," he told Tate.

Tate cast him a puzzled look.

"Your father and I talked today an' he gave the go-ahead on your brothers an' the girls getting together."

"Huh—that doesn't have anything to do with me," Tate huffed.

"It's hard tellin' what Jenny has heard. She works for them an' I'm sure they don't want to lose her. Maybe they got wind you were taking her with you, and realized the best way to keep that from happening is to break you two up. An' I bet my socks Jenny thinks I talked Klas into it." Blackwood nodded with conviction, his face etched with irritation.

"It was my brothers that badgered him," Tate said, with reproach. "But she wouldn't believe I had anything to do with that...naw...do ya think...?" He sounded skeptical, but his perception was keen. "She's jealous. She thinks I'll make a bid for a night's frolic with one of the other girls."

"I'd wager on it. Maybel can be damn convincing." Blackwood pursed his lips and nodded.

Tate studied her in the flickering firelight as she bent to peer in the pot before her. Holding a spoon in a sure hand she vigorously stirred the ingredients. "She sure don't hold back when she's mad." His tone sounded lighter. "If she don't boil me with supper, I'll corner her later an' make her listen."

Klas leaned forward, his brows raised. "Did you figger it out, son?" He smiled slyly.

"Yeah, Pa, I think so," Tate grumbled, his eyes sweeping over his brothers. "All any of you had to do was tell me. You all knew why Jenny was in a snit." John, Tad, and Jim tried to affix innocent expressions on their faces as Tate scowled at them.

Blackwood pulled a sack of tobacco from his vest pocket and began to build a smoke. "Well," he said, hesitating a brief instant while he raked his tongue across the cigarette paper and twisted one end. "I should have mentioned it when I sent John back from point"—he reached for a smoldering twig to light the cigarette—"an' I reckon I almost knew Maybel or one of the other girls would pull something like this." He exhaled a cloud of smoke. "But it's not easy to always remember how much deviltry a woman can stir up."

"Well, Jim could have said something when he ambled out an' hung around while I did all the tendin' to the stock. But...nooo...all he did was stand around with a shit-eating grin saying it's gonna be a great night." Tate then shrugged, saying with a resigned attitude, "Oh, well, guess I'd be doing just like them if the shoe was on the other foot."

Tate and Blackwood watched Jenny walk toward them with two plates piled high with food. Quickly they both stood. It was the stomp of her feet or the hostile set of her shoulders that told them if they continued sitting they might get a lap full of supper.

Her eyes turned to ice crystals as she shoved Blackwood's plate in his hands. She thrust Tate's plate at him, saying, "I hope you choke."

"Do you know, you're pretty even when you're mad." Tate's tone said it was more a fact than a question. Meeting her glaring eyes, he continued, "We still have to talk, there's a couple things I want to clear up."

She responded with a venomous squint, swished her skirts about, and marched away.

Wilma hurled a cold mocking glance in Tate's direction as she instantly fell in beside Jenny. She put her arm around Jenny's shoulder, patted, smiled, and began talking to her in a conspiring manner.

Blackwood watched with narrowed eyes, his astute mind busy unraveling a new concept. Perhaps the solution to the mystery of who told what to Jenny was not Maybel after all.

Chapter Fifteen

THE CHILL OF the hour before dawn caused Blackwood to shiver and sent him deeper into his bedroll for an extra measure of warmth. Still weary he hung drowsily in the region of neglect with his thoughts rambling. Maybe I'm too old for this, he pondered, then quickly dismissed that idea. His meditations drifted from his bad timing in crossing the trail of the girls, causing him a delay, to his annoyance at himself for not participating in last night's activities. The Ericssons sure enjoyed themselves. They kept him awake most of the night with their clumsy tramping about. Right away, knowing this was envy rearing its ugly head, he drew on the honesty within himself and admitted they had been notably quiet. Unable to let go of all his irritations he muttered in a thick, sleepy voice, "Shit." His ears then picked up the sound of light footfalls moving in his direction. Good, he thought, it's about time someone remembered me.

"Blackwood, you awake?" a soft voice whispered. "I brought you some coffee. It will be dawn pretty quick and I'd like to talk to you before anyone else gets up."

Talk? he asked himself. What the hell for? It's better I save my breath for breathin'. But he uttered gruffly, "What's to talk about?"

"I know you're still mad," the soft voice continued, "an' I don't blame you. I shouldn't have sloshed the hot coffee on you an' Tate."

These words brought his mind out of its sluggish state. "Jenny, what're you doing here?" He opened his eyes and sat up. "What's wrong?"

"I wanted to let you know I'm sorry about the way I carried on at supper last night." She handed the cup of coffee to him and paused while he took a swallow. "Tate explained everything an' I've 'bout decided to go with him today when we part company."

The uncertain ring in her voice prompted Blackwood to quickly say, "Don't sound like you're too sure about leaving. Don't go if you don't want to."

"That's not what's bothering me. I do want to go." She fidgeted for a bit then asked if she could sit down.

Blackwood shifted so she could sit at the foot of his bedroll. "Tain't no problem, then. Just go if you want." His voice lapsed into silence while he tried to make out the expression on her face in the darkness. "Is there something else you wanted to talk about?" he questioned as she arranged herself, facing him.

"I don't rightly know. Guess it's mostly a feeling I have."

"Sometimes feelings are powerful. But if that's all you got, it's not much to go on," he said, taking another drink of the coffee.

"Only other thing is, I overheard some snatches of talk." The alteration in the pitch of her voice told him she was having trouble with the admission of listening to another's conversation. "I know I should have minded my own business, not listened, and probably shouldn't be bothering you, either." Her voice faded as she hung her head. "But I heard my name," she blurted out, raising her chin. "An' what I heard together with what Tate told me, about them maybe not wanting me to leave, has set me to thinking."

Blackwood, not being long on patience but doing his best, urged her to tell him what she overheard. "If your name was spoken, I suppose you have the right to know why. Ain't the least bit use of you fretting about it. So spit it out, let me judge if it's a worry."

A big sigh escaped from her that said it was a relief he didn't think she was a busybody, and perhaps he could allay her sinister feeling. "Last night I was so mad at you an' Tate, I couldn't sleep. You know Lily, Wilma, an' me sleep under the wagon?"

Blackwood nodded. "I know, to keep Lily an' Francine apart."

"Anyway, I wasn't in bed long before Lily got up an' left. Soon's she's gone Wilma called to me, soft like, but I didn't wanna talk so I pretended I was asleep. Wilma then gets up an' calls to Maybel, an' she don't call her Momma like usual, just Maybel."

"Is that so strange?" he asked.

"I've never heard her call her anything but Momma." She hesitated. "But I guess not. Anyway . . . when she said, 'Maybel, get your ass out here,' that was sure not usual." Blackwood could sense Jenny squirm and almost see her blush as she rushed on. "I've never heard Wilma cuss and her voice sounded kinda funny." The next few minutes hung silent.

Finally, he said, "Is that it?"

"No. I heard Maybel ask where I was, an' Wilma told her I was asleep. This is the part... that...upset me." She stumbled about for the right words. "Wilma said, 'I'm warning you, Maybel, if you don't keep that goddamn dirt digger away from her, there'll be plenty bad trouble, a knife-in-the-gullet kind, and you know I ain't foolin'.' Maybel started into shushing her, they moved away, an' I didn't hear any more."

"Hmmm, are you sure 'knife in the gullet' is what you heard?" Blackwood's mind back-tracked through all she had told him.

"Yes, I'm sure. But I must have heard wrong, don't you think?" Her voice held a pleading quality, almost begging him to say she had mis-understood. "A short time after Wilma an' May-bel left, Tate called me and we went for a walk by the stream. When I got back Wilma was still gone but Lily was there. I told Lily I was going with Tate the next day." She fell silent for a moment, reached for the cup and asked, "Would you like more coffee?"

He waved her hand away. "Have you told me everything?"

"Yes." She sighed then added, "Lily told me if I was smart I wouldn't tell anyone I was going, just up an' go. But I can't do that."

"Did you tell Lily an' Tate what you heard Wilma say?" The first streaks of light were be-ginning to hint of daybreak, and he could make out the troubled expression on her face.

"No, I just couldn't. Wilma has been so good to me, I owe her a lot." Hesitating a moment she fussed with her hair then continued in a hollow voice. "At first I figgered, when you only hear parts of what someone else is saying you can get the wrong ideas. But the more I thought about it the more I worried. Guess I just needed you to tell me it's only foolishness."

"Here." He handed her the cup. "Why don't you go ahead an' start breakfast. We don't want to cut out of here too late. I'll be there in a minute to get some more coffee." His words came out overloud. He had spotted movement among the trees in the low brush and knew they were being watched. Gripped by the seriousness of the situation, but not wanting to alarm her, he lowered his voice, making it affable. "You go about as usual, don't say anything about what you've told me, and above all don't worry. Everything will be all right."

Blackwood rolled out from under his blankets. After strapping on his six-shooter, he grabbed his towel, casually flung it over his shoulder, and headed up through the trees toward the stream. With the lack of light in his favor he had only a few yards to walk before he could circle back to search the area. It took scarcely a moment for him to position himself where he could overlook the camp and hear anyone moving around or near his bedroll.

His eyes restlessly searched through the brush and trees in the direction of the wagons. The only sound that cut the air was the breeze rustling the leaves, so he bent to inspect the ground for tracks. Suddenly, with senses honed fine, his scalp began to crawl and the hair on the back of his neck stood on end. Slowly he pulled the peacemaker from its holster. Hearing his name being called distracted him and he shifted his head hard to the right. He saw Cora, approaching his bedroll.

Within a split second before a solid object collided with the left side of his head, he heard its *whoosh* part the air. As he had drawn his pistol at the first prickly sensation his instant reaction set off one wild round. The impact of the blow pitched him to his knees, the world turned dark gray. Blackness folded in on him.

Chapter Sixteen

BLACKWOOD SAW DAWN'S pink streaks were beginning to fade and full daylight was taking over as he regained consciousness. Cora was bent over him, bathing his face with a damp cloth. The Ericssons and the girls were standing over him, excitedly demanding to know what happened.

"I thought I heard an animal sniffing around,

drew my gun, then I heard Cora call. I raised my head to answer her an' must have moved too fast, buttin' my noggin on a tree limb." It was the best he could come up with on such short notice. He silently thanked Cora for calling out to him. If he had not shifted his position to answer her, he would be lying on the ground with a split skull, instead of a lump on the head.

Cora placed her hands on his shoulders as he started to rise and cautioned him, "I don't think you should be in too big a hurry to stand. You have a goose egg there, cowboy." She gingerly touched the side of his head. "Also, you're bound to have quite a headache."

"You're right. Maybe I should stay put for a minute." He looked up at them, his face expressionless. "You all go eat so we can break camp, otherwise it'll be noon before we get on the trail." Struggling, he made it to a sitting position. "Klas, if you don't mind I'd appreciate it if you'd hang around—I just might need a little help. Cora, if you would stay an' keep moppin' with that cool cloth I'd be beholden."

Blackwood watched the others go until they were out of hearing range, then turning to Cora he fired off a couple questions. "What did you hear? Did you see anything or anyone?" He carefully picked himself off the ground while he waited for her answers.

"Only thing I heard was your gun fire." She looked uneasy and Blackwood got the idea she was holding back.

"That's all you heard, an' you saw nothing?" He stared at her, trying to make her out.

"That's right." Her answer was curt while her eyes strayed from his face.

Deciding to try another tactic he came up with, "You like the life you lead an' wouldn't want to do or say anything to cause a problem between you an' the other girls, right?"

Her eyes did not stray this time; they blazed right into his as she took an angry step forward, hands on hips. "I have never said I liked this life. I have lots of young brothers and sisters at home and a very sick father. What I do puts food on their table." Her green eyes shot sparks and her red curls bobbed up and down as she nodded to emphasize each word. "Besides, I said I saw nothing. And the only thing I heard was your shot, a scuffling noise, and somebody running."

Blackwood saw her attention was drawn toward the wagons and knew she had nothing more to say. "Awright, go on an' help the others." Anyway, he considered, it wasn't wise to keep her too long and have someone wondering why.

After Cora left Klas confronted Blackwood. "Why don't we bring this out in the open?" he demanded, a sharp edge to his voice. "You and I both know which one of them gals is tall enough an' I bet strong enough to pack a wallop like that." He pointed to Blackwood's head.

Blackwood touched the lump and winced. His head was beginning to throb. "Simple, she's a woman an' I'm trying to avoid problems. Besides, are you plum sure? I'm not. Could have been any one of them, except Cora." He swept his hand toward the wagons and the campfire.

Klas stiffened and sputtered, "You ain't suggesting...you think...one of my boys—?"

"Hold on," Blackwood interrupted. "That's not what I meant. I was bending over checking for tracks when I was hit. So you see it could have been someone not too tall. But we can rule out Cora an' Jenny." He had not considered one of the Ericssons but now that it had been mentioned, and not of a mind to overlook anyone, he wondered where they had been during the ruckus.

"Sometimes I jump too quick," Klas admitted. "Jenny was pouring coffee for me an' my boys when we heard the shot, but I don't rightly know where the rest of them were."

Blackwood willingly took his word and double-checked on his knowledge of the whereabouts of the girls. "You didn't see Maybel, Wilma, Lily, or Francine?"

"Nope, they weren't near the campfire an' I don't remember hearing them in the wagon." Klas pursed his lips, looking thoughtful. "When everyone ran up here to see what the shooting was about they came from all directions."

Blackwood's brow furrowed. "We best get to the vittles an' clear camp. We've wasted enough time on this." He went to his bedroll, neatly rolled and tied it. Hefting it under his arm he moved to walk with Klas.

Klas took a slow, deep breath as if he weren't ready to let go. Turning to Blackwood and seeing his set face he gave in. "Suppose you're right. Let's go."

Together they went for their morning meal. Klas quietly plodded ahead. Trying to ease the jolt to his head Blackwood walked lightly and let his weight down gently. His thoughts were already busy on a plan that would enable Jenny's leaving with Tate to go smoothly.

Blackwood led the way as they moved into the group. Everyone was silently huddled over their plates, overly engrossed. Jenny approached, her face mirroring uncertainty. She halted in front of them, offering each a plate of food.

Klas accepted his with a simple, "Thanks," then moved to join his sons on the other side of the campfire.

Blackwood's thoughts went over the morning's conversation with Jenny and once again the strong antagonism he felt toward Wilma rose up in him. And it was this that made his eyes narrow as he unconsciously peered in the direction of her and Maybel.

Time was running too short to linger over coffee but they listlessly sat about sipping from or peering into their cups.

Jenny rose, picked up the pot, and broke the silence. "More coffee, anyone?"

"Here, let me." Maybel hastily took the pot

from her. "This is the last go-round so if you want some hold up your cup."

Blackwood's gaze followed Maybel as she poured out the portions. When Wilma held out her cup he saw Maybel pour something more than coffee in it. She had added a liquid from a small vial hidden in her free hand. Watching intently he was certain Wilma was the only one to get the extra something with her coffee.

Maybel became highly agitated as his eyes bored into her. He was certain she knew he had seen her pull her sleight-of-hand trick. She tried to cover up by commencing to point out to the girls their duties in breaking camp. "You all fetch the paraphernalia to me." As her nervous, high, unnatural voice caused heads to turn toward her, she self-consciously cleared her throat, then lamely continued. "I need to rearrange things in the wagon."

At that point Blackwood became hard aware that this would be a first for Maybel—to actually participate in the labor. Previously she had been successful in giving the impression of working but had merely dictated orders.

When Maybel approached Blackwood, sitting off to himself with his back braced against an imposing cedar tree, she asked in a solicitous voice, "Are you feeling better?"

"Fair to middlin'," he said with a shrug. He sensed from her sober manner she realized he was suspicious of her. Had he made his feelings too obvious? His mind raced. Perhaps she had a logical reason for slipping something in Wilma's coffee. After all is said and done, Wilma is her daughter. So now he searched for something to say that would break the strained silence and also sound amiable. "If I was bound to abuse myself, I guess my hard head would be the best spot to pick."

"Yes, I can agree with that." There was little warmth in her tone or the glance she gave him.

A rebellion rose in him and he said, "Look, Maybel, let's stop beating around the bush." Glancing at her he found her face set. "Jenny is leaving with the Ericssons today....I want no trouble...an'...." His voice faded.

She soberly said, "I know about Jenny, but go on."

"I intend to make short work of any difficult situation." His voice held a mixture of warning and promise.

After eyeing him a moment she coolly asked, "Whatever gave you the idea I would make trouble?"

Carefully he thought out his argument, slowly drawling, "Does Wilma take medicine in her coffee? Or was it something else that went in her cup?"

A shocked look swept across her face then slowly she relaxed, and finally shrugged, trying to achieve an air of indifference. "Wilma is... not well but she...won't take her medicine. So I sneak it to her in her coffee...she is none the wiser. An'...I would just as leave keep it that way." She was stumbling over her words and staring at him intently. "She...had a bad night an' I suspect she'll...uh...sleep most of the day."

He was almost sure she was lying. And he was positive this morning was the first time he had seen her dose Wilma's coffee. Having no recourse but to accept her explanation he reiterated, "Just remember. No problems with Jenny's leaving."

Before the deep timbre of his voice died she turned, giving him a scathing look. "Jenny is like a daughter to me. You don't even know her." She deliberated a moment then with a sting in her voice concluded, "Wilma thinks of her as a ...sister....We girls want what's best for her."

"Sometimes Wilma is a little too overprotective. Wouldn't you say? Or do you call it sisterly?"

"An' just what does that mean?" Her eyes blazed with outrage. "I'm sorry I hired you," she spit out bitterly as the color drained from her face.

Chapter Seventeen

"THAT MAKES TWO of us." Blackwood matched Maybel's harsh tone. He was as close as that to telling her she could have her money back. He was of a mind to ride out when the girls' images swam before him: the brave squaring of Cora's shoulders declaring she had taken over the responsibility for her family; Lily, striving to find an easier life than she'd had on the poor dirt farm; Francine's smiling lips and cold eyes, far out of her depth on this stretch of empty land. Even Maybel crossed his mind with her harebrained idea of becoming a grand madam when she opened a fancy bordello near the San Francisco Bay. The only one of the girls he could not get worked up over was Wilma, and he felt she would survive in a pit of snakes. He was trapped, he could not just walk away. Instead he became frustrated and thought of the dangers that could befall the girls because Maybel had persuaded them to join her. "Tell me, Maybel, why in God's name did you risk such a long haul without hiring someone at the onset to guide and protect you?"

"I got my reasons." She sent him a haughty look. "Besides, 'twasn't any trouble to get to Independence, then we were with a wagon train to South Pass. After we left there we met up with some soldier-boys out of Fort Henry going to Fort Hall an' tagged along. Not long out of there, we met up with you." She tilted her head over a raised shoulder at a jaunty angle, as if she were one of the smart people in a world of dummies.

"This ain't getting us anywhere. Let's get the hell out of here." He stood, pitched the cold coffee and sediment out of his cup onto the ground. "Let's head 'em out," he shouted and raised his arm, circling it over his head.

The low murmur of conversation stopped as everyone hustled to break camp.

Blackwood was heading toward the grassy meadow where the animals were hobbled but stopped short when he saw Maybel helping Wilma to the wagon. Wilma stumbled and sagged, she was beginning to collapse.

Moving to help, he asked, "What in the hell is wrong with her?"

"I told you she wasn't feeling well," Maybel said testily as she propped Wilma against the wagon.

"Climb in the wagon an' I'll boost her up."

"No, no, I can handle her. Come on, honey." Maybel put her arm protectively around Wilma. "Help Mamma get you in the wagon, dear. I've made a nice pallet, you can lie down."

Wilma ignored Maybel, looked at Blackwood with bleary eyes, mumbled incoherently, and jabbed at the air with her fist.

"Get in the wagon, Maybel," Blackwood ordered as he turned Wilma to face the opening then bent to put his shoulder under her buttocks to heave her up.

Maybel scrambled up and took hold of Wilma's arms, pulling as Blackwood pushed.

"Jesus H. Christ, Maybel, you should stop feeding her so much. She's as weighty as any man."

He did not see the startled look Maybel threw him.

Wilma continued muttering, then clearly said, "Ah shit," and laughed uproariously.

Blackwood's expression did not hide his contempt. "She sounds drunk to me."

"That's crazy," Maybel rapped out and again put her arm around Wilma, cooing soothing words as she turned her toward the inside of the wagon.

Blackwood shrugged, retrieved his saddle and bedroll, then moved on to his horse. The piebald was full of hell and did not want to be caught and bridled. "Damn you, get that hind end over here," Blackwood cussed, then made the click sound that brought the black and white into line. "I don't need your sass this morning, got plenty others laying guff on me."

"Got you talking to your horse, huh?" Klas grinned. Not expecting an answer, he looked up at the cloudless sky and remarked, "Looks like another warm day."

"Yup," commented Blackwood, half listening.

"I'll ride point with you." Klas mounted, sitting easy waiting for Blackwood. "Jenny has all her belongings in our wagon. Tate is handling the team. Jenny an' Sonja'll be riding with him. Guess we're ready when you are."

Now it was time to pull out. Blackwood's eyes probed the area, taking in the beauty of the grassy meadow, tall trees, and the abundance of free-flowing water. "Feast your eyes, Klas. It won't be this way much longer, civilized man is moving in. Trees will be hacked down and the ground plowed 'fore ya know it." He lifted his hat, ran his fingers through his hair, then settled the hat firmly back on his head. "But I reckon that's called progress." He swung up on the back of his pony and moved out ahead of the wagons.

Klas knew his remark was not meant as a disparagement of him and he took no offense.

They rode side by side, each hesitant to disturb the silence. Blackwood built a cigarette, struck the big lucifer on the heel of his boot, and took a long pull, blowing the smoke into the clear morning air. Klas knocked his pipe on his boot, tamped tobacco in the bowl, and started puffing it into life. This gave the erroneous appearance they were out for a Sunday ride to enjoy an after-breakfast smoke, but the next words they spoke belied this calm impression.

"Know anything about this trail I'm gonna take? Anything I should watch out for or...?" Klas's voice drifted off.

"Very little. I've been in the Utah Territory but

farther southeast than the Applegate Trail. Did a little wrangling down thata way when I was a boy. That's where I met up with ol' Stace, he weren't no marshal then. But what do you want to know? I might of caught some hearsay an' will be glad to pass it on." Blackwood turned a grave face toward Klas.

"I'd be obliged for anything you could tell me. Oh, I got maps an' I listened careful to that feller that came to church an' gave his spiel on what a paradise the valley is, an' how easy it is to get there, but..." Klas paused to puff vigorously on his pipe and a swirl of smoke rose from the bowl.

"Let me think on it a minute." Blackwood furrowed his brow as he rifled through his memory for any scrap of information he had heard. "Don't nothing helpful come to mind. Everything is kinda sketchy. Far's I know you take the trail to Mary's River which is a far piece. Then you follow along it skirting around a few pretty good-sized hills till you leave the water behind." Topping a knoll, Blackwood reined up and sat in contemplation. Spread before him were verdant rolling hills with tall wild grasses swishing back and forth to the whim of the breeze. What an eyeful, he mused, quiet and peaceful with only solitude missing. He swallowed the thought, nudged his horse forward, and continued giving Klas rough details of the trail as best he knew. "I understand farther south water becomes very precious, but like I said somewhere along that trail you come to that river. Seems to me I also heard you have to keep an eye out for the Digger Indians along that riverbank. They steal cattle after nightfall. But don't know if that's true, it's just something I heard a time back. 'Course it's always wise to keep an eye peeled for Indians. We ain't having trouble out here like they are back there"—he motioned toward the east—"with the Hunkpapa. But you never know when a raiding party might jump you." Blackwood paused, raised his head to scan the horizon. "It should be a pretty well marked trail. I believe somewhere in that neck of the woods is also Fremont's Trail. He was by that way in forty-five, I think. You won't have too much trouble if you keep your wits and mind the water." Winding up the lengthy speech he felt he had used enough words to cover a month's worth of talking.

Klas took a moment before responding. "We've been preparing for this journey for over two years. Don't intend to lose any cattle to Indians, an' we got lots of good strong water barrels. Took a deal of pain in choosing what we needed for this trip, right down to those rifles my boys carry. In fact a friend put me in touch with this feller in Connecticut that made them rifles. Took him a time to get 'em made. Claimed he was going in the business of selling. But for now, my boys have the only ones."

Blackwood had spent only a couple days in the company of the Ericssons but he knew they were not foolhardy. They had come more than twice the distance they had yet to travel, and their condition was as good as if they had been on the trail for only a few weeks. Blackwood allowed the difference was in the planning, as opposed to just throwing everything in the wagon and hitting the trail.

A long time ago he had educated his eyes, ears, and nose for the remote frontier life. His eyes now told him they were closing in on the Ericssons' turnoff. He could see the difference in the sway of the grass at the divide, when the breeze bent the lush carpet of green. They would part in less than a half hour.

Chapter Eighteen

KLAS AND BLACKWOOD trotted their horses a few yards beyond the split in the trail, drew to a halt, and dismounted. Blackwood thrust out his hand. "We best make our farewells short," he suggested. "We both have a pretty good patch of ground to cover before nightfall."

"If you're ever in the Umpqua Valley region go

north a hoot-an-holler to the Willamette Valley you will find us near that river with our door open and a pot of java on." Klas grinned, shaking hands with him.

They finished acknowledging it had been a pleasure to have made the acquaintance of each other when the wagons approached. Blackwood led his horse off the trail and motioned Lily to push on.

Lily waved goodbye to Klas as she passed and kept the mules moving up the trail. Francine, Maybel, and Cora crowded the opening at the rear of their wagon, throwing kisses at Jenny and the Ericssons.

To Blackwood, the day looked bright; brighter than it had in a while, and he attributed this to the slick way Jenny departed. Proud of knowing his mamma did not raise a fool, he was certain the potion Maybel had slipped Wilma was directly responsible for Wilma quietly resting in the wagon when the time came for the parting of the ways.

Cora moved forward to join Lily, as Francine settled in the wagon for a nap.

Maybel stood with her head against the edge of the rear opening staring at the speck on the horizon that had been—but a short time ago— the Ericsson wagon. Slowly turning to peer into the dimness she glanced at Wilma sleeping peacefully. A guilty sensation washed over her, immediately replaced by a sense of foreboding.

When...why...had her life taken this turn? Closing her eyes she let her thoughts drift back to the time when she had been a young carefree girl.

It began with a quarrel she had had with Daniel François Aubber. Hesitating, she searched her memory but found she could not recall what had caused the dispute, only that she had wanted desperately to make him jealous. To achieve this she indulged in a wild fling one evening. Her unrestrained flirting and wanton ways placed her in an extremely unpleasant situation with an unfamiliar group. By the next day she realized she had made a grave mistake, and vowed to reform. But it was too late; she soon found she was in the family way.

When she confessed to her father she was going to have a child, he, a bitter, devious, and power-hungry man, demanded she claim the chief official, Daniel's father, took advantage of her. He said he would attest that M. Aubber came to his home, found her alone, and seduced her.

His intention was to blackmail M. Aubber, thus intimidating a strong adversary and perhaps coercing his way to great power. She had wavered, but her feelings for Daniel were strong, and knowing it was her own stupidity that had placed this problem on her shoulders, she could not bring herself to ruin Daniel's family. When she refused her father simply opened the door, banishing her with only the clothes on her back.

Losing all track of time and sense of location she wandered the streets of New Orleans. Unknowingly she strayed into New Orleans's red-light district. Consumed with fear and desperate for a moment of rest away from the watching eyes of the street vermin, she searched for a place to hide. Spying a likely spot, she quickly ducked through a wrought-iron gate leading to a narrow passageway, adjacent to a large pink door. Unaccustomed to the harsh life on the streets, her mind and body succumbed and she fainted at the entrance to the garden of a notorious house of ill repute. The Pink Palace. Cora, a very young painted lady of the evening, found Maybel. Cora was touched with pity for this older girl and nursed her back to health. After a few days, when her condition improved, Cora induced Madam Durban to visit.

Struck by the girl's unusual beauty Madam Durban asked her to work at the Pink Palace. Not knowing of another alternative she accepted. Cora and two other whores, Lily and Francine, became her friends while teaching her tricks of the trade along with the house rules. In a short time she knew she liked the whores' way of life. Daniel's image faded and died.

When she became too large to work, they gave her lying-in time, with a promise she could return after the birthing.

As her time grew near she made arrangements to be attended by a midwife and stay in the country home of a town doctor. Complications developed and the midwife went into town to fetch the doctor. A fierce spring storm blew in, delaying their return, and she was alone when Wilma was born. Frightened, but having seen the birth of animals and armed with the information the midwife had passed on, she had no choice but to attend to herself. It was much too early for the baby to be born. Fortunately, contrary to what the midwife feared, it turned out to be an easy birth and no problems developed. No, no problems developed, she thought, only a deep, dark secret I dare not even think about.

Shaking herself, she momentarily interrupted her musings about the past. A loud sigh escaped her lips that would have been heard by Lily and Cora if Lily had not taken that moment to shout at the mules.

Shifting position, Maybel let her mind drop back in time again.

Madam Durban welcomed her back, saying, "Because the baby is a girl, she is also welcome to stay at the Pink Palace and we all look forward to raising the child." The girls were eager to help, but she would never let anyone touch or care for the infant. In time, the whores got used to having Wilma around but ignored her.

Although reasonably happy she was also a woman with ambition, and began to dream of a beautiful burgundy and gilt house of her own. She imagined the talented and exotic girls she would have working for her. Besides the lovely girls to take care of the customers, she would provide plays or song and dance entertainment, even gaming rooms for the gamblers. "Oh yes!" she often told herself. "My house will far surpass anything the Pink Palace has to offer."

Soon she began to hear stories of men in the gold camps of the West paying exorbitant sums for a woman. Knowing it would take far longer than she cared to wait to earn the money for her own house, she started developing the idea of working these mining fields as she traveled West.

When Madam Durban began to come down hard on her to start Wilma on the road to prostitution she became panicky. She decided to persuade Lily, Francine, and Cora to go West with her and share expenses. This idea wold make it possible for her to leave sooner. The girls fell in with her plan, embracing it as a good scheme.

Wilma hated Maybel's way of life and, when they were alone, she constantly harped at her to give it up. They had many a bitter quarrel after she had been with a man.

She tried in vain to explain the new plan to Wilma. But after realizing Wilma would not accept one house of prostitution for another, she fabricated a story, telling her they would be working for money to buy land to settle on and live the rich, full life of ranching.

Everything had been moving along according to plan when a tragedy struck, and she knew it was time for them to leave. One early morning two of her best-paying customers were found dead. One was discovered in a back alley and the other in his carriage.

She was upset but unconcerned until she found the blood-spattered dress under Wilma's cot. She knew Wilma had not been injured, but fearing to learn the full truth yet knowing she must, cautiously questioned her. With a faraway look and a strange smile Wilma told her she had gotten the marks on her dress while playing a new game. She taunted her with the names of the two dead men, and told her how much she enjoyed the new sport and thought she would continue playing it.

Chapter Nineteen

WAS THIS CHILD she loved beyond reason merely trying to frighten her? She had been shattered and tearfully implored Wilma to stop making up such wild stories. When Wilma saw the fright and love in her eyes she fell into her arms, sobbing, "Forgive me, Mama. Please forgive me. I love you." Worried, she again placated Wilma with descriptions of how wonderful the trip West would be, all the while beseeching her to be a little more patient.

Shaking herself, she tried to come back from the past, as if that had been the complete account and all had ended with a weepy understanding between mother and child. But she knew this was not true. Too many unexplained incidents had happened since leaving New Orleans. With that her thoughts skimmed over some of the puzzling events, then rested on crusty ol' Clyde. He was a harmless old mountain man she met in Independence. Due to his help they were permitted to travel with a large wagon train to South Pass. How he had loved to sit around their campfire, telling tall tales and sipping coffee. She thought of the fun she got out of teasing him, in a bawdy sort of a way. He never did more than pat her on the rear end. At the time she felt it strange that three days before reaching South Pass his horse bucked him off and dragged him for over a mile. He was dead when they found him. Again, she asked the same question she had asked many times, why would his gentle old nag, owned for over ten years, suddenly decide to get rank?

She shuddered, then silently criticized her thoughts. What the hell am I trying to do? Conjure a mysterious death for everyone that ever came near me? Opening her eyes she swore to handle whatever came her way. She would take a step at a time and not dream up trouble. She also resolved to tell Blackwood she was the person who hit him, even though she wasn't. Perhaps if she apologized it would bring harmony and keep him from casting a suspicious eye every time a twig snapped.

Dreamily, her eyes focused on the horse attached to the rear of the wagon. Suddenly she had an idea. Wilma didn't know how to ride. Perhaps it would keep her mind off Jenny if she used her energy learning to handle a horse. She decided to ask Blackwood, before suppertime, if she could have the horse.

A feeling of relief surged through her. She had been more than a bit anxious, but now she felt sure mastering the ability to ride would use up Wilma's energy with little time left to brood.

Becoming aware Lily was calling her she lifted herself out of her reverie. Making her way to the front of the wagon, she asked, "What is it?"

Cora turned to answer for Lily, but seeing the drawn look on Maybel's face, she exclaimed, "Are you all right?"

"Of course I am." She leaned forward. "Why did you call me?"

Lily motioned ahead to where Blackwood topped the ridge of an arroyo, riding full-out toward them. She pulled up on the reins to slow the mules. "From the way he was waving a minute ago I had the impression he wanted us to wait for him here. Maybe we should." She looked questioningly at Maybel. "What do you think?"

"Yes, by all means stop." Maybel's expression changed to alarm. "Wonder what's put him in such a rush?"

Without wasting time by stopping to give them information, as he drew near Blackwood motioned for them to follow him off the trail. Lily feathered the ribbons, turned the mules, and fell in behind him toward a brush, cottonwood, and willow area with a sheer ridge at their back. The position was an excellent vantage point. It was a stronghold with a large amount of deadfall, for use as cover. A trickling stream was skittering nearby.

Swiftly dismounting he said, "Grab your rifles. All of you get to the mules and put your hands over their muzzles so they won't whinny or bray. You can ask questions later."

He led the piebald farther back into the trees, slid his rifle from its sheath, and hurried back to the girls. After a quick explanation he took up a post ready for action.

The waiting was making them edgy but it wasn't long before they saw in the distance the faint outline of riders. Without appearing to be in a hurry, the riders made their way up and down the folds of land, drawing nearer.

Blackwood's eyes scanned the not-too-distant slope they were due to top within a few moments. As they came into his view he took in their dark flowing hair, fine physique, colorful beaded buckskins, and breathed a surprised gasp. "Damn, Crow, what they doing this far outta their territory?"

As the small party crested the hill to the west they halted their horses, their eyes probing the land stretched out before them.

Blackwood knew they saw the wheel marks the wagon had made when it left the trail and he tensed with apprehension. Glancing at the girls, he saw their uneasiness, and caught their attention with a motion not to fire until he gave the signal.

The warriors drew together, making considerable movements with their hands and much talk. Abruptly they spread out and slowly advanced, their rifles held across their arms at the ready. There were five of them, each leading two fine-looking horses. But one was having difficulty staying atop his pony.

Blackwood searched his knowledge. This was Shoshone Territory. The Crow were from the Northeast and it was unusual for them to stray this far west of the Bannocks. They were also noted for their horsemanship and would go to any length to obtain a good horse. They must have been on a raid, he decided, and captured the horses they were leading. But why so far from their home? And didn't they know this was a supply road and they could run into a column of soldiers?

The injured warrior lifted his head and Blackwood recognized him. Yellow Hawk. A strong but young brave he had been on friendly terms with in the past. He had no urge to let Yellow Hawk know about the soldiers he might encounter on this trail for his first duty was to protect the girls and he would not dare expose them to the danger. Yellow Hawk was filled with bravado but unpredictable. He also had a feeling this lot was attempting to get to their own land, by the shortest route, and might not provoke a fight. Yet he knew enough not to underrate them and allowed as how they would also not run from a fight unless they were hopelessly outnumbered. Indians were a shrewd but curious people and it was wise to never underestimate their intelligence or cunning. And never ever figure you knew what they were going to do for they would undoubtedly do just the opposite.

Blackwood decided to play his hunch, stay under cover, let them pass, but keep a sharp eye out to make sure they did not double back and attack.

At a quarter mile away the five slowly moved across the grass-bent trail the wagon had made. Not one warrior glanced at it or to where Blackwood and the girls were hidden among the brush and trees.

Cora, standing behind a breastwork of fallen timber and brush, closest to Blackwood, breathed relief. "Whew, they didn't even see where we left the trail."

"That's a foolish remark," Blackwood whispered. "They not only know where we are but how long ago we left the trail an' no doubt how many in our party. I just hope to hell they don't know you are women." As an afterthought, but most important to them, he added, "An' I'm keeping my fingers crossed they are in a hurry to get their wounded leader, Yellow Hawk, back across the Rockies."

Cora looked startled. "You know him?"

Blackwood nodded. "We know each other."

"Well, if you are a friend of his, we don't have anything to fear. Do we?"

He gave her a sharp look. "I didn't say we was blood brothers. We was just friendly a time back. If he knew there were five women and only one man, I really don't know what he would do. It's best we sidestep it if we can."

After warning the girls to stay put and alert he silently moved out. Snaking his way to higher ground he kept the warriors in sight.

He saw them stop and hand the lead lines of the horses they had in tow to Yellow Hawk. Yellow Hawk was wounded, but not as badly as he first appeared. He now sat straight and seemed to be giving instructions to the four braves.

Blackwood snorted in disgust and checked his weapons. Now he had to think. What would they do? Would they angle back to ambush him and the girls? Indians feared and hated an ambush but used it at every opportunity.

Chapter Twenty

BLACKWOOD WORKED HIS way under the trees and around the edges of the thick brush. Carefully, he avoided the tall grass, which would move when he crawled through it and betray his presence. Silent as a falling snowflake he crept cautiously to a better viewing and hearing location. Getting as near as he dared, he hunkered down to watch and listen.

Combining eloquent speech with sign, Yellow Hawk's hands moved in quick, short strokes as he issued orders. Suddenly, he threw the lead lines on the ground, motioning to the braves to secure the extra horses. While they were busy with this, Yellow Hawk tapped his heels against his horse's belly and shifted to the front position.

A stretched stillness enveloped them as Blackwood intensely watched the Indian leader. His gaze seemed to cross the space between them, and Yellow Hawk jerked his head to peer in Blackwood's direction. Had the Indian felt his intense gaze—had he stared at him too long? Cautiously lowering his eyes, Blackwood prayed for the moment to pass. His luck held when the silence was broken by one of the braves continuing to grouse. While the Indian leader was distracted, he stealthily wriggled backward to safety, on his elbows and knees.

Blackwood was thankful he understood sign, and glad he could speak and interpret the Crow dialect. "Awright, Yellow Hawk," he whispered to himself, "if a fight is what you want, we'll be ready for you." He quietly but swiftly made his way back to the makeshift fort.

As he was swallowed by the deep shadows of the heavy growth, he called softly to the girls and cautiously entered the thicket. He swiftly set them to the task of fortifying the small area. Cora secured the mules and the two horses to large tree branches in the center, to keep them from bolting when the shooting started.

Their time for preparation ran out and Blackwood settled everyone down to wait and watch. His eyes raked the patch of ground before him, not even a twitch in a blade of grass escaped his attention. He did not see anything, but he knew they were slowly moving nearer.

Uneasiness crawled over him like a family of ants making their way across his body. They are horsemen and no doubt they will attack on horseback, he speculated. Straining his ears, he heard their advance. When they drew near he shouted, "Here they come," and rifle fire exploded to his left. He half turned and heard one of the girls scream as two more rapid shots pierced the air. A warrior broke through the brush directly in front of him. He fired and saw the brave catapult from his horse, dropping lifeless not twenty yards away. The remaining braves suddenly veered away, breaking off the attack.

From the corner of his eye, he saw Lily leave her post, running toward Maybel, screaming, "Maybel's hit."

"Get down," he yelled, "or you'll be next."

She quickly dropped beside Maybel.

Giving Francine a quick glance, he saw her face was set, her eyes narrow slits. "Come on, you red devils." Her rifle was held to her shoulder at the ready.

Two warriors abruptly burst forth to his right, followed immediately by the other two on the left. Their whooping cries filled the air.

Blackwood jumped quickly to the area Lily had left vacant when she ran to Maybel, his rifle spitting lead to cover the move. Rolling behind a large dead log, he heard the near whiz of a bullet, then felt a burning sensation along his shoulder. He gave it little attention. He was too busy. A brave was nearly on top of him. Raising his gun to fire, he saw the Indian go down—one of the girls had tagged him.

When the three remaining warriors moved hell-bent out of rifle range, Blackwood called to the girls, "Hold your fire, men."

Yellow Hawk and his three braves turned to make another sweep. Blackwood, filled with anger, wildly raged, "Give it up, Yellow Hawk. Take your men home."

Yellow Hawk drew to a halt, motioning for his warriors to do the same. Sitting on his horse ramrod straight, he stared fiercely toward Blackwood. "Who calls my name?"

"Me, Blackwood," he shouted. "Many moons ago we were hunting partners."

Yellow Hawk's braves boisterously protested, but with a flick of his hand he silenced them. One brave, not wanting to be denied the opportunity to count coup, continued to urge his horse forward. Perhaps his dreams had shown him he was a mighty warrior possessing strong medicine this day and he would have scalps to decorate his lodge. But his leader gave a sharp command that quickly brought him back in line.

"Why you wait to greet me as friend?" Yellow Hawk asked, his face unreadable.

"You kept me kinda busy. I didn't have a chance till now." Blackwood stood, motioning to the girls to stay hidden. For a long moment they looked at one another. Showing no fear, but knowing Yellow Hawk was a proud man, Blackwood picked his words carefully. "I know you are a great distance from home. If you want to collect your fallen braves and be on your way, we won't fire on you. My men and I have no quarrel with you, but if you want we can finish this. It don't make no never mind to us."

Vehemently, the aggressive warrior again tried to influence Yellow Hawk to continue the fight. Yellow Hawk raised his hand with forceful dominance and little talk to his men, and gave his answer. "No! They are not to be harmed. Blackwood is friend. His word is good. We get braves an' go home."

The truth, thought Blackwood, is you don't know it was girls that put up the good fight. You lost two men and you know we lost only one or perhaps ours was just slightly wounded. And that puts the odds in our favor. But aloud he said, "Don't take more than one of you fellers to pick 'em up."

He then told the girls to continue to hold their fire, while emphatically motioning for them to stay well hidden.

After collecting their dead, Yellow Hawk turned his horse to face Blackwood. "We will meet again," he signed.

Blackwood wondered if he meant they would finish this at another time or they would meet on friendly terms. But he signed, "May your medicine be strong all your long life."

When the braves were out of sight, Blackwood cautioned the girls to hold their positions. Mounting his pony, he followed to make sure the hostiles departed. He watched as they gathered their horses and headed homeward. Now his thoughts turned to the girls and he was anxious to get back to see how badly Maybel was hurt.

As he entered the thicket, Cora and Francine gathered around him, both talking at the same time. Quieting them, he confirmed the Indians had gone, then asked about Maybel.

"Lily said she was shot in the shoulder. It was a crease with no bullet to remove, a clean wound an'—" Cora ceased talking as Francine broke in. "She lost some blood but she'll be fine."

Lily approached with Maybel in tow. "Thank God, Blackwood, we had you with us," Maybel said as Lily hugged him. "What's this...?" Lily quickly withdrew her hand. When she saw her hand covered with blood, she gasped, "Lord's sake! you're hurt."

Chapter Twenty-one

BLACKWOOD FLEXED HIS shoulders and a sharp pain streaked across his back. "Can't be much or it'd been givin' me fits 'fore now." He'd forgotten that near miss, in the heat of the battle. Absently removing his hat he ran his fingers through his hair. "We'd best hitch up an' lite a chuck."

"We are not moving one inch until I take care of that wound." Cora turned stubborn and pointed to a large log, ordering, "Sit down an' take off your shirt."

Keenly aware they should be on the move he said, "It can wait till later." It was anyone's guess how long Yellow Hawk could keep the warrior with the dream of counting coup in line. And he knew he could not rule out the chance they might see something along the trail that would tell them it was women with him. No Indian would take kindly to the idea of losing a fight to a group of women. They would be honor bound to return.

"Come on, it won't take but a minute," Lily coaxed as she handed Cora a washpan of water and some bandages.

"Awright, but you better do it in jig time. We got to get the hell out of here."

Cora helped him remove his shirt and held it before her. "Would you look at the size of that hole?" she said, putting her fingers through the ripped fabric. "But I think it can be fixed."

"Let's see." He took the shirt from her. "Damn it all to hell. Do you have any idea how much that shittin' shirt cost?" He inspected it a moment then rolled it in a ball and threw it on the ground.

Lily grimaced and snatched it up. "Cora said she thought it could be fixed."

"You're lucky it was mostly shirt that was damaged," Cora scolded as she washed the wound in the cool water. "Hold still, I want to pour some of this on it." She then splashed liquor across his shoulders.

"Why the hell are you wasting good whiskey like that?" he said, wincing. "It would feel a damn sight better in my belly."

"I don't doubt it for a minute." She grinned, pouring a little more over the wound. "But that wouldn't keep you from getting an infection." The trickle of blood subsided as she applied the bandage. "We'll change this a couple of times an' you'll be good as new in a few days."

While Cora helped him put on a wrinkled but fresh linsey-woolsey shirt, she commented on how lucky they were the Indians decided to leave. Each girl confessed that in the middle of the fight they thought they were done for. The ordeal they had gone through showed in their stance and could be heard in their quiet voices.

Ignoring their talk, Blackwood eyeballed Maybel, wondering if she had looked in on

Wilma. It grew quiet. The girls followed his gaze, puzzled until he asked, "Where's Wilma?"

"Oh, my God," Maybel exclaimed, breaking into a run toward the wagon unmindful of her wounded arm. She stopped short as she approached and stared wide-eyed, her hand shooting over her mouth. Blackwood and the girls followed behind. The women gasped as they took in the sight of the wagon. It had been mottled before with pink, white, and red petticoats stretched across the top; now it was also riddled with bullet holes.

"It must have taken all the wild shots. But looks to me like they are too high to have done much harm. I'll give it a look-see." Blackwood climbed onto the wagon. Turning, he looked at Maybel. Her eyes were rapidly blinking, bravely holding back tears. "You stay with the girls, I'll see if she's all right," he told her.

Spying Wilma's figure outlined in the dim interior he made his way to her pallet. He started to kneel beside her when a hand was placed on his shoulder. Maybel was behind him. Letting her hand rest there a moment longer, she said in a soft, pleading voice, "Please, let me."

Easing himself out of her way, he swung nimbly off the back of the wagon.

For a moment the only sound was the whisper of the wind twisting around them. The girls stood stunned, wide-eyed, waiting. Finally Maybel's tinkling laughter pierced the silence. "She's fine. She slept like a baby through the whole thing."

Yeah, thought Blackwood, a baby until she wakes—then she turns into a giant pain in the ass.

The heat grew more pronounced as the sun reached its zenith, and Blackwood felt a stir of displeasure at having to return to the dusty trail. He found himself thinking how good it would be to stretch out under a shade tree and nap. But knowing they had lingered longer than they should, he whipped up action from the girls by telling them it was possible the Indians would return.

In a flurry, they were squared away and ready to get back on the trail. Still shaken, the women asked Blackwood to ride close to the wagon. Anxious to put as much distance as possible between them and the battle site, Lily snapped the whip around the ears of the mules. The lead mules knew this signal and stepped out in perfect unison. It was not a hardship for the animals to keep on the move because they had eaten and rested during the fight. While the wagon rolled, the girls prepared the noon meal from the cold leftovers on hand. Keeping up a steady pace it was conceivable they might arrive at the mining camp before dusk.

Lily, beginning to relax and feel out of danger, was startled when seven riders broke from the gully on her right. They were coming at her from less than four hundred yards away. Jerking back on the reins, she brought the wagon to a sudden halt. Jolted by the unexpected stop, loud cries of reproach came from the girls as they tumbled about in the wagon. Blackwood swiftly moved out from the left side. After cautioning the women to prepare for trouble and stay inside, he nudged his horse forward to confront the men.

Chapter Twenty-two

BLACKWOOD TOOK IN their grubby appearance; sweat-stained shirts, mud-spattered trousers, heavy worn boots, and floppy hats. Without question most were miners. Pulling up, the riders shouted greetings.

One whiskered rider, still wearing his apron, looked to be a shopkeeper. Appointing himself as spokesman, he nudged his horse forward. "We'uns heard the echo of rifle fire and we's expecting a supply wagon. Been having a mite of trouble with the Shoshone lately, an' had a idear the wagon was under attack. Ya know what all the shootin' was 'bout? I can't afford to lose them supplies." He took a breath, and cocked his head toward Blackwood.

The shopkeeper had good reason to worry

about the supply wagons for he stood to make a small fortune from the commodities he would sell to the miners. The average miner thought the supply of gold was never-ending and spent as much as a dollar fifty for a pound of flour, three dollars for a pound of brown sugar, or four dollars for a can of fruit.

"A ways back we had a skirmish with a small war party. But it's long over now," Blackwood explained, then asked, "Where'd you say you were when you heard the shots?"

"Up yonder." He made a sweeping gesture toward the high buttes, in the near distance. "All loud noises down here bounces off them thar hills. An' the racket is heard in Camp Precious." He pointed to the north. Grabbing a gulp of air he stared beyond Blackwood, then flashed a toothy grin and snatched off his hat.

The six other riders, hats crushed against their chests, swiftly moved their horses forward to stand beside the spokesman. Blackwood did not need to turn around to know the girls were behind him. The gleams in the miners' eyes were a dead giveaway. The corners of his mouth quirked as he backed his pony to one side. He made the introductions—"Ladies, these gentlemen are some of the good folks from Camp Precious"—and thought of how a man made a fool of himself over a female.

Maybel moved forward as the miners dismounted, jostling each other to reach her first. "Precious." She smiled and extended her hand.

"My, my, what a de-light-ful name for a minin' camp." Her Southern drawl was thick and gushy.

The miners quickly forgot about the rifle fire they had heard. They gathered around the ladies to persuade them to stop near Camp Precious for a few days. All volunteered to help set up a camp. By the time the wagon arrived at the outskirts of Camp Precious several more miners had joined them. There were so many helpers they were falling over each other.

Blackwood managed to corner Maybel and ask, "How's Wilma? You should try to keep her awake for a while. You must have overdone it with the laudanum."

Maybel started to protest but changed her mind, deciding to be honest. "I guess I must have. But my thoughts were only for her," she quickly added, then continued. "I knew she would be upset about Jenny's leaving an' I wanted to make it easier for her." She looked contrite, with her eyes cast toward the toes of her shoes.

It's fine with me, he thought, don't make me unhappy you saved us from having a big hooraw. But he gently touched her on the cheek and said, "It'll come out awright. I'm gonna scout around and see if I can't find a better top for your wagon." He moved off to take care of the piebald before giving his attention to the mining camp.

The late afternoon sun gave long shadows to

the trees and boulders as he ambled toward the ramshackle blemish called Precious.

He stopped to roll a smoke and give the make-shift place the once-over. With the exception of the general store, built of stone and equipped with an iron door and shutters, it was a hodge-podge of shacks, slapped up without much thought. It certainly isn't much to look at. I wonder if Sandy passed this way? he mused and thought of his true reason for going to Fort Boise. Sticking the cigarette in his mouth he scratched the sulfurhead on the heel of his boot and cupped his hands around the flame. He took a long draw and located the bar and card house about midway down the dusty street. Just on the outside chance he might pick up some infor-mation on Sandy, or some of the gang he ran with, he decided to ramble toward the saloon and gaming establishment. Later he would check on a top for the girls' wagon.

He noticed the place, aptly named "Saloon," was constructed of canvas, logs, and about any-thing else the builder could lay his hands on. What a sorry sight, he thought. He shouldered his way through the open door and moved to-ward a bar that was a plank supported by large barrels. He ordered whiskey. "Leave the bottle," he told the barkeeper and slapped a double eagle on the bar.

He knocked back the shot, poured another, and turned to survey the room. Being the only watering hole around it was occupied by miners and drifters. A few rickety tables were scattered about to accommodate any unfortunate card-player willing to lose his poke to a tinhorn in a game of faro or three-card monte. In one corner, plunking away on the keys of a rinky-dink piano sat a large fat man wearing a porkpie hat.

Blackwood heard someone at his elbow clear his throat, then a voice said, "Say, ain't ya the feller come in town with them pretty gals?"

Blackwood glanced out of the corner of his eye at the weathered old man.

The stranger gave him a snaggletoothed grin and asked, "Do ya think ya could get that pretty little redhead to—?" He clamped his mouth shut sudden like when he saw the flat, cold look in Blackwood's eyes. "I didn't mean nothin', mister." The grin dissolved as he backed away. "Jus' tryin' to be friendly," he muttered and scooted out the door.

"Sonovabitch," grumbled Blackwood to himself. "I've done about everything, but be damned if I'll drum up business for whores."

The barkeeper, seeing the look, said, "Pay ol' Seedy no never mind. He's harmless."

Blackwood let his eyes drift over the barkeeper, a powerfully built man with a straight-forward look about him. "Guess I must have mistook his meanin'. I only work as a guide for the ladies."

"I figgered as much," he said, and looked

Blackwood over, much the same as he had been sized up. "Dan is the name." He held out his hand. "I own this eyesore."

"Blackwood," he said and gave Dan's hand a firm shake. He hesitated, then knowing a saloonkeeper would be his best source for information, asked, "Any chance you've seen a feller answers to the name of Sandy—about my size with a bushy beard an' long sandy-colored hair? Could be he passed this way some time back."

"Take your pick." Dan waved his arm, taking in the whole room. "No barbers here-about and just 'bout everyone wears a beard an' long hair."

"You wouldn't mistake him for one of these men." Blackwood glanced around the room. "The Sandy I'm talking about is trouble, an' wears his pistols crossover."

"Ah, a shooter." Dan raised his brows. "Let me think on it," he said, and moved away toward a drifter making a racket at the end of the bar.

The small saloon began to fill; word had spread that women were in the area.

It was true, there were men who would ride far just to hear another's voice. Some miners worked for many months, from dawn till after sundown, with only themselves for company. Most would not leave their claim unguarded, if it showed color, for fear someone would take over their digs while they were gone. It was a lonely, back-breaking life and a sparse amount of men who came from the East did not have the

sand to take the hardships. Those who recognized the row was too hard for them to hoe
packed up and made their way back where they
came from. Others, not willing to face their family and friends as failures, lingered on. And
there were always the few who decided to ride
the owlhoot trail. Not every owler riding the
outlaw trail was crooked or murderous; some
took up that life because of unfortunate circum-
stances. But many were just downright mean,
only wanting to live by the iron they carried on
their hip and happy with the power or riches
they thought it would bring.

The girls were a big drawing card, and this
was the mixture of men beginning to find their
way to the only saloon between Fort Hall and
Fort Boise. News of this sort traveled fast and
soon Precious would overflow its boundaries.

Dan moved about lighting the lamps. They
made a circle of light in the middle of the room
but left the corners dim.

Blackwood spied an empty table at the edge
of the room with a chair backed into one of the
large logs holding up the canvas top. It would
do just fine; from there he could see all comings
and goings. He picked up his bottle.

After a few minutes, Seedy sidled through the
door, clapped his eyes on Blackwood, and gave
him wide range as he made his way to the bar.

Blackwood watched as Dan said a few words
to him, then handed him a rag and a broom.

Huh, a swamper, thought Blackwood. That's losing your touch when you can't read a body better than that; but on the other hand it's the first time whores have hired me, and it could be I'm just a mite touchy about it. He began to wonder what Seedy had wanted from Cora and made up his mind to find out. He caught his attention and motioned to him.

"Yez sir, ya wanna see me, sir?" Seedy was cautious.

To put him at ease Blackwood said, "How in tarnation did this place get a name like Precious?"

"They tell me there was this feller everyone called Old Doc Toomie. He had some diggin's just a few steps from where you're sittin' now. He kept saying the country here 'bouts was almost as pretty as his wife, Precious. The name seemed to catch on an..." He shrugged, then asked, "Can I do anything else for ya, mister?"

"I'd be obliged if ya could round up some grub for me," Blackwood said, pouring himself another drink.

"Dan has an ol' Indian cook, she's not bad at it neither, an' most times she has some stew an' leather bread. Ya want I should brung ya some?" A big grin spread across his face; he had expected to be clobbered.

"That'ud be awright, then you can tell me what you wanted from that little redhead."

"Oh, 'twern't nothin'." He nervously twisted

the rag in his hand. "I'll get ya grub." He scurried away, but was back within a few minutes with the food.

"Did ya want some hot coffee?" Seedy asked.

"Nah, I'll jus' stick to this." Blackwood touched the bottle. "But I now figure you can say what it was you wanted from the redhead." I hope to hell it isn't what I'm thinking, he said to himself, but I'll set him straight fast enough if it is.

"Ya know how 'tiz...I don' really need it... but..." He hemmed and hawed around the answer.

Blackwood had been forking food in his mouth but now laid the fork aside, swallowed, and gave him his full attention. "I figure it's time to get it said."

"It's that red hair, if'n I could jus' have the tiniest lock of it." He spoke rapidly, looking hopeful.

"Well, I'll be...A lock of her hair is all ya want?" He almost laughed. "I don't know if she'll want ya to have it, but I'll ask her." He shifted his attention across the room to face a young man at the end of the bar. He nearly dipped his head in recognition, the feeling was so strong he knew him, but checked himself in time. The look he received in return was not friendly; in fact, Blackwood read a cold, sinister disdain in the young man's eyes.

Chapter Twenty-three

EARLIER THAT EVENING Maybel had struggled to wake Wilma by urging her to get up and walk about. Wilma opened her eyes, wrapped her hands about her head as if it were throbbing, and closed her eyes again.

"Come on, dear, it's time you woke," Maybel repeated, maneuvering her to a sitting position.

"Where are we?" she mumbled.

"Near a mining camp," Maybel answered, placing a damp cloth on Wilma's brow. "You should really try to get up an' move around some. We're camped in a divine wooded area an' I know you would enjoy exploring it." She was concerned. Could Blackwood be right? Had the dose she gave her that morning been too much?

Wilma raised herself on an elbow. "Whatsa matter with me? I feel awful."

"You've been ill. You're still a little woozy but you'll be fine shortly. Here, drink this." Maybel held a cup of coffee to Wilma's lips.

Time whiled away as Maybel continued to mop Wilma's brow and talk in a low, soothing voice. She dared not leave her until she was fully awake.

After more than an hour had passed, Wilma sat up on the edge of the pallet. "Well, I must be getting better 'cause the hammering in my head has finally slowed down." She stood in the center of the wagon where she stretched her arms over her head, and said, "I sure do feel rested."

"That's good, dear." Maybel pulled her back down on the pallet beside her. "I brought you something to eat. You'll feel even better after you get something in your belly." She filled the spoon with food, holding it out.

Wilma took the spoon and reached for the plate of food. After studying her mother a moment she asked, "Why is your arm bandaged? What's happened? Where's Jenny?"

While Wilma ate, Maybel took her time telling about the Indian attack. She praised Blackwood's strategy, told how brave the girls had been, and explained why her arm was in a sling, carefully avoiding any reference to Jenny's leaving. She made it sound as if two days instead of one had passed.

The fog appeared to have completely cleared from Wilma's head as she asked, "How long did you say I've been sick?"

Sticking to the story she had concocted Maybel cautiously said, "A couple days."

Wilma sat several minutes, her head cradled in her hands, elbows resting on her knees. Twice she twisted her head, giving Maybel a peculiar look. Finally she spoke in a cold quiet voice. "Awright, you've beat around the bush long enough, don't you think? Now tell me about Jenny."

Wilma's tone startled Maybel. The first time

she'd heard that inflection in her voice had been after the slayings in New Orleans. Trying to be gentle, she explained that Jenny had gone with the Ericcsons. She also made a special effort to convince her it would be a ride of at least five or more days to catch up with them. "That is, if a person could even find the trail the Ericcsons took," she added, in hopes of discouraging Wilma from going after them.

Wilma sat quietly, absorbing this information. Suddenly she began to shake, then something seemed to snap within. Her expression turned so savage Maybel could not believe it was the same person. "Is Blackwood in camp?" Wilma snarled.

"No, he left to find a top for the wagon."

As Wilma fixed her gaze on Maybel, an odd little smile appeared on her lips. There was no warmth in the smile and it failed to lessen the strangeness in her eyes. Abruptly she raised her fist, and without warning knocked Maybel to the floor. Bending over her she glared with uncurbed hate, her fists clenched. "You...you... are evil and unclean. I tried to save you, but I knew that that last night at camp with the Ericcsons you were beyond my help. Blackwood an' your filth caused Jenny to leave. She was pure. I tried warning Blackwood, too. I sent his horse to him at the water hole the first night he joined us. I also hit him that morning, but he didn't take heed. Now you an' him have to be struck down." She twisted her head as if listening, then hissed "Fact is, you and Blackwood plotted from the start to make Jenny leave me. I hate you. I'll take care of both of you—an' he comes first."

"There is no plot. I'm your mother. I love you and have always tried to do what was best for you."

The racket was audible but the words were not clear and it startled the girls, who were standing several feet away. Cora ran to the wagon. It was too dark to see inside. She cried out, "Maybel, is everything all right?"

Maybel quickly answered, "Everything is fine, I jus' lost my footing."

"Is Wilma awright? Would you like some help?"

"No, no, Wilma is still not feeling too well but I can manage."

The interruption quieted Wilma. She told Cora in a cold voice, "She only fell. Go away, don't bother us." When Cora moved away Wilma turned on Maybel once more. "I don't ever want to be called Wilma again. My name is Wilbur, understand? I want to hear you say it, go on, say my name." He began to pace in the small space the wagon afforded.

"My dear, I've explained many times why we've had to pretend you're a girl. If anyone at the Pink Palace had known you were a boy, they wouldn't have let me keep you."

He seemed unaware of her comments as he

said, "You don't have to be a whore, but you like wallowing in slime."

"I don't know of any other way to earn a living."

"I don't want to hear any more of your lies. Do what I told you, say my name."

"Wilbur," Maybel said, rising to stand unsteadily, facing him. She was frightened by the unnatural look in her son's eyes, but made a feeble attempt to placate what she hoped was anger. "I only called you Wilma with the thought I was doin' what was best for—"

Not listening, he broke in. "I'm a man—so start treatin' me as one," he hissed through clenched teeth, and puffed out his chest as if he had attained a new power. He stopped pacing and raised a fist at her again, declaring, "I should kill you, right now."

Maybel was stunned, but she loved her son and held on to the idea that this too would fade with time. She pushed her fear aside. "I agree, this would be a good time to start calling you Wilbur." Trying to divert his attention, she cheerfully said, "I have a good idea. How would you like to have that horse?" Maybel pointed out the rear of the wagon, where the sorrel was hobbled. "An' you could learn to ride." The smile she turned on him was weak.

Giving her a sneer he turned to rummage in a trunk. "The boots an' clothes I bought a while back are in here, right?" With a groan he lifted his hand to rub his forehead. When Maybel didn't readily answer he shot her a glance, saying bitterly, "Well?"

It was on the tip of her tongue to tell him not to look for the clothes. But not missing the stiffening of his face she became wary. "I put them on the bottom, but don't you think you should rest until your headache goes away?" she said slowly.

He didn't answer and the silence between them grew ominous.

"Find the shears," he ordered. "I'm gonna cut my hair."

By the time he finished making the transformation it had grown dark and the girls had gone inside the shack.

As he jumped off the tail of the wagon he staggered, winced, and put his hand to his head again. Maybel followed, believing she should do something to stop him, but with nothing coming to mind she simply begged him not to leave.

"Jus' shut up an' keep ya trap closed about me leaving camp," he snarled. "You think I don't know how to ride. Well, I do and can saddle a horse, too." He gave a demented giggle. As he swung aboard the sorrel he asked, "Which way did Blackwood go?"

"I don't know." She shrugged, then pleaded, "Please don't—"

"Quit sniveling an' remember what I told you about not tellin' anyone I left camp. I'll be back an' take care of you later." His look was threatening as he jerked the horse about.

Maybel's eyes traveled over him, beginning to get an inkling of some of the peculiarities she had missed. She turned back to the wagon, her head bowed, in deep concentration.

Not knowing one horse from another himself, Wilbur didn't realize most men knew a horse and its owner by its markings. Feeling sure that he and the horse would not be recognized, he used the saloon noise as a guide and slowly rode toward it.

Chapter Twenty-four

SEEDY WAS SO grateful to Blackwood he made a pest of himself by stopping at the table every few minutes to see if he could fetch him something. Blackwood started to ask him if he knew the young fellow at the bar when a noisy pair of miners came through the door, distracting him. When he looked again the young man was gone.

An uneasy feeling gripped Blackwood as he thought of the youth's gnawingly familiar appearance. He was of slight build, fine features, and dark hair chopped off just above his plaid shirt collar. His gray plainsman's hat had been pulled low on his brow, making it impossible to see his eyes. The uneasy feeling deepened as the image sharpened in his mind's eye. Blackwood realized with a start that he felt, more than actually saw, the menacing look the young stranger had passed him.

He sat staring into his glass a few more moments. Deciding he could use some air he pushed to his feet and made for the door. As he stepped toward it he heard a sneering remark. "Must be a dandy, no one in their right mind would wear a getup like that." The comment, loud enough to reach Blackwood, came from one of three hard-eyed, reckless drifters sitting near the door. The familiar young stranger who had disappeared from the bar was seated at their table. They all had the earmarks of loud-mouthed bullies looking for trouble. They'll find it, Blackwood thought. If a man tries hard enough, he can find anything. He threw them a look that clearly sent the message, "Don't talk me to death, make your play," and held his hand over the butt of the gun hanging low on his hip. Could be he was just the person to show them the error of their ways. On the tail of this thought he recognized it was the liquor driving him, and it would be a mistake to make a dangerous play guided by drink. He would wait and see if they pressed him. Slowly he stepped to the outside. No comments followed.

Peering about in the darkness he saw a few dim lights winking from the windows of the shacks that lined the street.

He hadn't gone much more than twenty yards

when he was startled by the quick movement of a shadow across the street. Damn, he thought, now I'm jumping at shadows.

A sense of peril seized him as he shook off the feeling that eyes were boring into him. Drawing the conclusion that it was a putrid night, he decided to walk off some of the whiskey, see to his pony, then bed down.

He stepped in front of a dimly lit window and fell to one knee, then all hell seemed to break loose. "Godammit," he swore. He had lost his balance when he stepped in a chuck hole made by a harsh spring rain. More than likely it had saved his life for he instantly heard the report of a pistol and the thud of a bullet as it struck a post above him. He rolled to a crouch, drawing his side arm. Still crouching low he swung around behind a shack. Running to the next opening he quickly made his way between the shacks to the front. Cutting across the street he moved to the rear of the building and up to where he had seen the shadow. He stopped to listen. All he could hear was the noise from the saloon. Whoever had taken the shot at him had made tracks. He was alone on the street, plenty worked up and cold sober.

The way he had it figured the saloon was the most logical place for whoever had taken the shot at him to duck into. If they had hotfooted it out of the area, he would have heard the crunch of footsteps on the rocky paths or the hoofbeats of their departure on horseback.

Blackwood was not the typical cowhand, though he had done his share of riding for the man. If there were a few steps to take him where he wanted to go, he would usually take these steps instead of climbing on his horse and riding. But now he wished he had his pony under him to make quick work of the short distance back to the saloon.

As he came abreast of the hitching rail in front of the bar, he recognized one of the horses. It was the sorrel he and the girls had brought in tied to the back of their wagon. The horse now belonged to Maybel. He had warned her it might be a stolen horse and she could be asking for trouble, but she had been willing to chance it.

Moving to just inside the door he quickly swept the room with his gaze. He looked for one of the girls who might have ridden the sorrel to fetch him. But what was more important at the moment was anyone that had the restless look of having rushed in from the street. If anyone is so much as breathin' hard I'm gonna call 'em out, he swore.

He elbowed his way through a cluster of men standing around quenching their thirst, making remarks about the women in excited voices, and casting sly looks at each other. They all had the same itch.

When he bellied up to the bar Dan greeted him. "Ya look like a wildcat with a sore tail." He grinned but his eyes were serious.

Blackwood's face held the expression of a determined and fierce man. "Tell me which one of these yahoos' jus' came in." He couldn't keep the challenge out of his voice.

"Someone did stomp on your tail." Dan squinted at him.

"It's jus' that I don't take too kindly to being shot at," he said harshly.

"I thought I heard shots, but it's so damn noisy in here I wasn't sure. Didn't nail ya, did he?" Dan looked him over.

"Nah, but it was too close to suit me."

"Well, let's see, the best I can come up with is about four, maybe five, that came in." Dan pointed them out to Blackwood, then moved down the bar to wait on a demanding customer. When he finished with the customer he moved back to Blackwood. "Here, have a drink, you look like you could use it." He poured him a shot. "There's one more that came in a few minutes ago. See that kid in the gray hat with the three toughs near the door? I 'member seeing him go out but he's back, so musta come in in the last few minutes."

Beginning to simmer down, Blackwood turned to look. It was the young man he'd seen earlier at the bar, but he didn't see anything out of line. The four were sharing a bottle and had their heads together, talking. He shrugged, saying, "Can't go accusing someone that cussed calm," and turned back to Dan, whose eyes narrowed as he stared across the room. "Those three, with the younker, have done nothin' but stir up trouble since they hit this camp," Dan snorted. "There's usually a fourth"—his face held a sour look as he continued—"an' looks to me like that young feller—he's new in camp—is of the same stripe an' throwin' in with 'em."

Remembering the sorrel tied outside, Blackwood asked, "Has anyone been in here lookin' for me?"

"Nope, not that I know," Dan said and moved away a few paces to serve a miner.

As Seedy walked by he collared him. "Did ya see who rode in on that sorrel tied out front?"

Seedy shook his head. "Didn't pay no 'tention."

Maybel must have loaned or sold the horse to one of these men, Blackwood thought as he glanced around the room.

"Ya know," Dan said, peering at Blackwood. "Come to think of it, that other feller who usually hangs around with that bunch"—he moved his head slightly toward the group sitting by the door—"sorta fits the description of the man you're lookin' for, 'cept he's almost a head shorter than you, an' his sandy hair an' beard ain't all that wild. But he does wear his pistols crossover."

Chapter Twenty-five

INSTANTLY ALERT Blackwood started to ask more but Dan had moved a few steps away to give Seedy a piece of cardboard and a broom. "Here," he said, "sweep up some of that mud an' cigarette butts. It's startin' to hide the floor."

Seedy bobbed his head and sent a long glance and an open grin toward Blackwood.

For a lock of hair I've made a friend for life, thought Blackwood, as he gave him a short nod.

"That ol' man has sure seen a lot of bad luck," Dan said, indicating Seedy. "He's a honest, good worker an' not too hard to have around." He offered Blackwood another drink.

"No, thanks." He waved the offer aside. "I don't wanna fuddle my head." Leaning forward he asked, "'Bout this other friend of those three?"

"Oh yes, well, he's almost always with them, but I'd guess..."—Dan temporarily broke off as he turned to replace the bottle on a shelf behind him—"he must be visitin' the girls an' will be in later."

"Think I'll hang around for a spell an' take a gander at him, if'n you don't mind?"

Dan's face turned gloomy. "Ain't hankerin' to have my place tore up."

"Ain't lookin' to start trouble, leastways not in here, Dan."

"Well, watch yourself. I seen 'em take a few

around here. An' I can tell ya right out they ain't new at the game." Dan moved a couple steps closer and stabbed his finger at him.

"Neither am I." Blackwood's voice held a grim note as he repeated, "Neither am I."

Time hung heavy for Blackwood as he waited. He was anxious to know if he would meet another member of a gang he had trailed for more years than he liked to think about, or if it was just another wild-goose chase.

"Don't that piano player know another tune?" Blackwood frowned.

"That's the only one he's played since he got here three months ago, so guess not," Dan said.

"Must be drivin' you crazy by now?"

Dan shrugged. "Nope, I quit listenin' 'bout two'n half months ago."

A loud bellow erupted as a ruckus started at the table of two time-worn miners. "'Tis too," one of them shouted. "'Tain't neither," the other one yelled back. They stood glaring at each other, then started swinging.

Dan cleared the bar by a foot as he jumped over it to reach the fighters. He grabbed them by the scruff of their necks, holding them apart. "All right, gents, shove along." He led them to the door. He grinned at Blackwood on his return. "It's all right, they're brothers, an' work a little hidden place in the hills. They get a small amount of dust out of it, and come here a couple times a week and after a few drinks start disagreein'." He reached for a bottle, held it toward

Blackwood, and poured himself a shot as Blackwood shook his head. "I'd offer you a beer if that
supply wagon 'ud ever get here. Supposed to
have a couple of kegs on it an' it's three days
late." Dan scowled.

Blackwood glanced over his shoulder and was
suprised to see the table empty that previously
had been occupied by the kid and the three saddle tramps. "Shit," he muttered and caught
Dan's eye. "Did you happen to see when the kid
and the others left?"

"Hell no, didn't know they were gone till right
now. Musta left when the brothers were raisin' a
stink." He looked around the room, then yelled,
"Hey, Seedy, come here."

Seedy hurried to Dan. "What's the matter?"

"No matter, jus' wanted to know if you saw
when the men sittin' at that table by the door
took out of here," Dan asked.

"Sure, I saw 'em leave. That other jasper
that's usually with 'em came to jus' inside the
door an' motioned to 'em to come outside. The
kid followed along. It happened when Jim an'
Art started havin' that little set-to." Seedy hesitated. "That all ya wanna know?"

"You didn't happen to see which way they
went, did you?" Blackwood asked.

"No." Seedy shook his head.

"Thanks, Seedy," Dan said, lightly patting him
on the back. "You can get back to work now."

"Well, hells-fire." Blackwood could feel his
riled blood begin to burn, checked himself and

cooled his temper. He figured that getting too worked up wouldn't help and only fools let their anger take over their control. Maybe dawn would bring better luck. He turned to leave. "Guess tomorrow's another day an' I can poke into it then. I reckon for now I'll see to my horse and get a little shut-eye. See you tomorrow, Dan."

Outside, he watchfully dodged to the rear, climbed to the high ground behind Camp Precious, and circled to approach from the up side the spot where he had stashed his horse and bedroll. It was a dark moonless night but the piebald picked up his scent and nickered in recognition.

He fell into the bedroll fully dressed, bone-weary, and was asleep before closing his eyes.

Just as quickly he was wide awake, wondering what had disturbed him, when he heard a whisper: "Here he is." Without warning everything happened at once. Rolling toward the whispering voice Blackwood grabbed for the legs to throw him off balance. As the body hit the ground he groped for the rifle he'd placed beside the bedroll before retiring. Coming up empty-handed he jumped to his feet, dodged behind a tree, and ran smack into someone. Swinging wild he connected with a nose and felt the blood spurt over his hand. He was then grabbed from behind, his arms pinned. Blackwood came down hard on a foot, causing the hold to loosen, then twisting around he threw a left hook, catching the assailant somewhere near the ear.

It was frustrating, fighting shadows in the pitch-black night, and Blackwood was losing ground. He couldn't tell how many were in this party but he knew there were at least three. One was on each side holding him while another used him as a punching bag.

"Ease up," said a voice to his left. "He don't want him killed. He wants that pleasure himself."

"I think it's best we get rid of him here an' now." The animallike growl came from the gent who threw the punches.

"I'm bettin' the dude who hired us to do this job wouldn't like it," a voice with a Texas twang warned.

The yahoo doing his damnedest to twist Blackwood's right arm out of its socket made it an even draw when he moaned, "Christ, I think the bastard broke my nose." His voice gathered anger as he continued. "I'm throwin' in with whoever is for killin' the sonovabitch."

Deadly time ticked by, then a slow, careful voice from the deep shadows said, "Not a good idea. I only pay for jobs that are done the way I want 'em."

Blackwood went down heavy as the two holding him let go.

The careful voice continued. "Tie him up. Take him to the place we agreed on. We'll meet later. I'll bring half the money, an' when the job's done the other half will be paid."

Blackwood was on the verge of oblivion, but a strong thought brought him around. Someone must have overheard him ask Dan about Sandy and this was a scheme hatched by that someone. It could be Sandy himself, for who else would be desperate enough to want him stopped from dogging their trail? The thought gave Blackwood new strength. He came up from the ground and staggered toward the voices. He heard, "Damn, there's no quit in him." Then he felt a blow to his head and everything went black.

Chapter Twenty-six

MORE THAN THIRTY years ago in Virginia, Seedy had been a family man and successful farmer. At that time he was known by his true name, Seton McClure. His red-haired wife and only child died from an illness friends and neighbors feared to be contagious. He became enraged when they wouldn't lift a hand to help and bitterly vowed to leave the area and never mix in another man's troubles even if his assistance would lighten the load. He had thereafter always looked the other way, but lately he had begun to hold this practice responsible for his run of bad luck.

Not believing he was too old to turn himself around, Seedy was certain he could change and advance to a better station in life through hard work, determination, and a little good luck. It was difficult not to bend to the old ways, and on occasion he would experience a slight fall, but mostly he took a stand. If he felt a wrong was committed, he opened his mouth and said so. No more would he drown problems with drink or move out of town.

In all the towns and mining camps he had left behind, while slowly trekking west, the people had looked down on him, calling him the town sot. Now they called him a cantankerous old man, but their voices held a note of respect.

As menial as his job was, Seedy regarded it as important. It was the beginning of a new way of life for him.

The Indian cook fed him and Dan let him sleep in the saloon, and his living expenses were therefore almost nonexistent, enabling him to save all his earnings. He had hopes of buying into a business or staking himself to a few months of prospecting.

Seedy worked hard and tonight like most times he was busy doing his chores.

After sweeping up the floor he dumped the debris in a box to be taken out back later, but on brief inspection he saw the spittoons needed cleaning. After placing a couple in the box with the floor sweepings he picked his way over a hundred yards in the pitch-black night, to the gully behind the saloon.

Bending to empty the box at the edge of the small ravine, he stopped dead in his tracks on hearing voices, and horses moving toward him through the brush.

In this part of the country nothing was taken for granted, so Seedy did not assume the voices were friendly. Instead he crouched low to watch and listen.

A voice came to him from across the gully. "I don't see what difference it makes when we kill him. Now or later."

"It don't make no never mind to me neither, exceptin' I want my pay for this job an' the only way we are gonna collect is to do what the man says. Soon's we get back to town we can collect half an' I for one am gonna visit the ladies."

Another voice with an edge to it growled from the blackness, "Will you shut up an' get on with it—let's get this biscuit eater locked in that shed. If we don't get shut of him soon, he'll come around an' start raising hell."

"You don't need to sound so all-fired dutiful. I heard this feller we got here was lookin' for you an' somehow I don't think it was for a game of—"

The voice with the growl broke in. "What you mean? Whar did you hear that?"

"You know that ol' coyote that keeps hangin'

around, sayin' he wants to ride with us? Hell, he
don't even own a horse, all he got is the rags on
his back an'—"

"Dammit, that ol' jayhawker ain't important,
jus' spit out how you know this here jasper was
lookin' for me."

"I'm tryin' to tell you what that ol' cuss told
me. He heard this feller here ask the barkeep if
he knew a Sandy and he described you to a tee."

"Probably wants to ride with us," he snarled,
but his voice sounded unsure.

The conversation made it clear to Seedy these
men were up to their eyebrows in something
crooked. He rooted himself behind a bush and
peered around it trying to catch a glimpse of the
riders on the other side of the narrow gulch. All
he could make out was five dark shapes—one
form seemed different until he realized it must
be a body tied across a saddle.

Seedy reasoned that whatever was afoot, four
of these horsemen were up to no good or they
would have brought the prisoner into camp and
announced the deed he had committed—or,
more believable, they would have killed him on
the spot.

It would be a fool's play and he would be
looking for trouble if he followed this outfit.
Well, trouble or not, it didn't seem to matter. A
man had to do what he had to, he admitted, as
he found himself stealthily weaving among the
brush and trees behind them.

Seedy became aware of the grave mistake he

had been making lately, by not carrying a firearm with him each and every time he left the
saloon. This was one of the first rules of sur-
vival. He had been lulled into a sense of security
by the routine of moving back and forth to the
gully dumping trash, and had violated this rule
of safety several times.

"Well, ya dumbhead," he admonished himself,
"since you're not smart enough to always carry
a pistol, you'll just have to come up with an idea
that won't involve shootin'." Snatches of their
conversation began to come back to him and he
knew they were not going to kill their prisoner,
at least not right away, and if they didn't hang
around after they locked him in the shed, he
could break the lock and set him free. If that
didn't work, well, he would face that when the
time came.

Keeping a safe distance behind the five horses
he occupied his mind with the lay of the land
and the direction they were going. When arriv-
ing in the territory he had taken the time to
comb the area, and had come to know every riff
and rill of the land, so it quickly became clear to
him where they were headed.

The only place in this direction where the
riders could take their prisoner was a played-
out mine about three to four miles out of Precious. He remembered that on one side, butted
against the hill, there was a small lean-to a
long-gone miner had built to store supplies. He
knew it was still there because he'd been tramp-

ing in the area recently when a sudden downpour caught him unawares and he had holed up in it.

Knowing where the riders were going gave Seedy an edge. He decided to go back to Precious, collect a shooting iron, and borrow a horse from Dan.

While he waited for the horsemen to get far enough uptrail so they wouldn't hear him hotfoot back to Precious, he heard, "I'm sure gonna hate to leave this prime piece of black an' white horseflesh. After I get paid for this job I think I'll just claim the hoss for myself." The voice held a note of arrogance.

Seedy knew full well who owned the mount.

Talk of the big black and white stallion had been bantered about camp as soon as the first miner returned to Precious, after helping the girls get settled. Now that he knew who these outlaws were holding prisoner, Seedy was all the more anxious to get to Precious, collect a firearm, a horse, and return to rescue Blackwood.

A notion lodged in his head as he headed back to camp. He had a hunch these riders were the same bunch that scooted out of the saloon when Jim and Art were having their squabble. "Don't jump to conclusions," he mumbled to himself. "Jus' cause ya don't cotton to 'em, ya don't need to tip the scales against 'em." But he couldn't shake the idea.

Chapter Twenty-seven

BLACKWOOD SLOWLY REGAINED consciousness and was immediately sorry. His body felt like it had been on the losing side of a tussle with a grizzly.

Making an effort to turn over he almost blacked out from the pain. He knew he was in bad shape as he collapsed on his back. There wasn't much of him that didn't hurt. Staring into the blackness he tried to get it straight in his head where he was and what had happened.

Running his hand down his chest and the battered area across his ribs to his hips, he found his leather cartridge belt and pistol missing. But his hand did not encounter a sticky substance, which meant there was no blood, so he hadn't been shot. The thought cheered him some.

Gulping too much air, Blackwood felt his ribs send waves of raw pain through him. But his memories began to unscramble. "The dirty sonovabitches held me while someone beat the livin' hell out of me," he said aloud. "Then one of the bastards must have laid their pistol upside my head." His anger mounted as details fell into place.

He moved his arm across the dirt floor until his hand touched rough wood. When he stretched his legs his feet collided with a barrier and he knew he was inside a small enclosure. With grim determination he pulled himself to the wood siding and to a sitting position.

A harsh crunching noise came from outside the shed. Whatever had caused the noise was now sniffing at the wood siding on the outer surface of the shelter near him. His first thought was that a wild animal had caught his scent. He had no idea where he was but his reasoning told him the area was uninhabited. They wouldn't have dumped him where he had only to shout and someone would come to his rescue.

Sitting with his back braced against the wall he breathed shallowly to lessen the pain. He could hear the muted sound of the wind rustling the leaves in the trees. This keen sense of hearing also told him the animal sniffing out there was alone.

His thoughts were busy when the snuffle turned to a soft neigh. Taking the chance they had been stupid enough to leave his stallion he made the clicking sound that summoned the piebald. He was instantly greeted with a comforting snort and a hoof pawing at the earth.

He had to get out of there. Agonizingly he wormed his way around the inside of the shed, looking for anything useful to free himself. He had found the door and was half senseless with pain when a new sound jerked him into awareness. A horse and rider were winding their way through the trees, drawing nearer.

The piebald greeted the newcomer with a soft

whinny. Blackwood could hear the creak of leather as the rider dismounted, and heard his boots strike the ground as he moved toward the shed.

"Blackwood, ya in thar?"

Blackwood told himself he knew the voice but his befuddled head erased the memory of it. He quietly moved his legs across the doorway. When he comes in I'll trip him, he thought as he gathered strength. A man's body can do many things when it comes to saving his life.

"This is Seedy. I come to help ya."

"I'm inside." His voice cracked as a breath of relief escaped him.

"I'll have ya out of there in a jiffy." Seedy grunted as he lifted the log jammed against the door and heaved it out of the way.

Blackwood had barely made it to his feet and was swaying precariously when Seedy forced the crude split-log door open.

"Haven't got a shot of rye, have you?" Blackwood asked, with a thread of humor in his voice, and was surprised when Seedy pulled a bottle from his hip pocket.

"Jus' one, then we better hightail it out uh here." He handed him the bottle.

"Thanks. I owe you." Blackwood lifted the bottle to his lips.

"Not me, Dan sent it. He thought ya might like a nip. I'll get your pony, then we better see how quick we can make ourselves scarce around

here." Seedy moved to the other side of the
shack and came back leading the piebald.

With the natural instinct of a survivor Blackwood tried twice to mount his horse. But with
each try the sharp agony punishing his sides almost made him keel over. He knew he had some
broken bones, and the only way he could get
himself in that saddle was if the stallion would
get down on its haunches.

Seedy saw he was in trouble and suggested,
"Get ya foot in the stirrup an' I'll give ya a
boost."

The effort proved too much for Blackwood
and he remembered only snatches of what followed. In a haze he recalled Seedy tying him on
his horse and leading him up a switchback trail.

He woke once to see gray streaks of dawn and
feel hands pulling and lifting him from the saddle.

When he came to again, he was lying on a
blanket, securely swathed in bandages from his
shoulders to his waist. He lay there for a time
before he became aware of smoke and the low
murmur of voices. Opening his eyes he saw tall
timber with old tree trunks and deadfall about.
There was a stream a few paces away and rock
walls on three sides. In one of the walls was a
cave with tailings near the entrance. It was twilight and the night promised a slight chill. He
turned his head to see silhouetted against a
bright fire a coffee pot and two men.

The gurgle of the stream made him conscious of how bone-dry he was, and after a couple of tries he got out, "Sure would appreciate a cup of that coffee." He struggled to rise on an elbow.

Both men jumped to their feet and rushed toward him. "Don't move," said one, then the other added, "You're busted up pretty bad an' if you move it's bound to do more damage. I'm Art an' this is Jim, my brother. Get the man a cup of coffee, Jim."

Their backs were to the fire with their faces in the shadows and Blackwood wouldn't have known which was which if the short one had not picked up a cup and moved toward the fire reaching for the coffee pot.

Art hunkered down beside Blackwood. "All your belongings is over there." He pointed beyond Blackwood. "You was raisin' such a fuss about your side arm, Seedy went an' gathered up all your things and brought 'em out here."

"Here, try some of this." Jim handed him the cup of coffee. "Must be hungry after not eatin' for a couple days. I'll see if I can't rustle up somethin'."

"My belly feels like it's been quite a spell since it had any grub but I ate last night, at the saloon."

Art gave him a long look then in a patient voice said, "You 'twern't at no saloon last night. Seedy come atotin' you in here night 'fore last."

Chapter Twenty-eight

A STIR OF surprise ran through Blackwood. It was difficult for him to believe two days had gone by. He shot Art a glance of disbelief, wrestling with the notion they might not be telling the truth. Finally he decided to accept their story for now because he couldn't come up with any reason they would want to lie. Trying to get a grip on all that had happened and give himself a little time to think, he asked, "Where's here, an' where's my horse?"

While the flickering firelight played across Blackwood's face he could feel Art studying him. With his eyes glued on Blackwood, Art rummaged in his pocket, pulled out his tobacco, bit off a chaw, and offered Blackwood the plug. Blackwood refused. Finally, Art appeared to settle on a decision and said, "This is the Art-Jim mine. My brother an' I own this claim. We don't cotton to letting strangers come in on us, but Seedy told us who you were an' we agreed to let you stay." Moving to the campfire he picked up the coffee pot and refilled Blackwood's cup. Squatting again, he continued. "For the time being I reckon you're safe enough here, and your stallion ain't far. He's just around that bend." Art pointed toward the other side of the campfire, then turning his head aside spit out a stream of tobacco juice. A short silence ensued as he rearranged the wad. "He's with our string over there where there's good grass an' water."

"I sure do thank you for going to all this trouble." Briefly deliberating, Blackwood then asked, "Did Seedy happen to tell you how he come to find me?"

"Yeah, he tol' us he heard them fellers out back of the saloon, how he followed them, an' found out it was you they had bushwhacked." His voice faltered and he ended up muttering, "An'...everythin'."

Blackwood had the feeling Art was holding back something. He wondered what "everything" meant but didn't press.

Jim approached, holding out a tin plate filled with a slab of side meat, a hard biscuit, and a heap of beans. In a not-too-friendly way he asked, "Is it true you're a outlaw an' pistoleer?"

Art gave a startled gasp and his eyes quickly cut to Blackwood.

In the quiet that followed, Blackwood was curious if that question was part of the "everything." Struggling to a sitting position, he tried to convince himself he didn't feel much worse than the times he woke from a night of fisticuffs and a good bit of town carousing. After taking the offered plate he answered, "Been a lot of things, pistoleer yes, but never an outlaw."

"Don't pay Jim no mind," Art said briskly. "He has a fool notion that anyone comin' near our mine is up to no good. He's always suspicious of everyone."

"That's awright, reckon most times it pays to not be too trustin'." Blackwood attacked the plate of food like a starving man.

Art stood, stretched, and yawned. "I think it's time we all got some shut-eye. Me an' Jim's day starts early. By the by, Seedy said he'll come out again tomorrow to see how you're doin'."

Blackwood grunted agreeably and sopped up the last of the juice on his plate. The food had been satisfying but the activity had taken a lot out of him and he welcomed the rest.

Setting the plate aside he eased himself down and lay watching the new moon cast slivers of light through the branches of the tall trees. Loneliness washed over him as he recalled the many nights alone on the trail when he was shivering cold or soaked to the skin and looking for shelter. A shack, a cave, or even a hollow log would have pleased him, and it would have been high grade if he'd had someone to share it with. Always being on the move, like a cloud crossing in front of a bright moon to new horizons, didn't give him time to make lasting ties.

His mind digging deeper into the past, he reminisced about the good times he'd had as a youngster on the Blackwood Ranch. He remembered his father discussing with him many long-range plans to increase their holdings, build up the herd, and divert some of their plentiful water supply to the drier sections. Think-

ing of his home triggered a blaze of anger at
how their plans and dreams had turned to dust.
The ignited fire within him grew hotter as he
thought of being near one of the men who could
possibly have been the one who raped his sister
or worked the action on the gun sending the
bullet to kill his mother or father.

While squirming to find a comfortable position, the beating he had taken two nights ago
came to mind. How they had kicked him again
and again while he was down. It was plain to
see he had to mend in a hurry and then by
damn he would go hunting. The men that
jumped him and the varmint whose voice he
had heard giving them orders from the deep
shadows would pay dearly for the discomfort
he felt this night.

Chapter Twenty-nine

DRAGGING HIMSELF out of a deep sleep Blackwood heard sounds coming through the earth.
He listened, and in another moment realized the
rhythmic thump was hoofbeats. All his senses
quickly became alert. Judging they had but a
few minutes before the horses would be upon
them, called to Art and Jim. Struggling upright

Art helped steady him while he buckled his holster around his lean hips.

The three were barely in position when they heard Seedy's voice call out, "Hello, the camp."

"Seedy, ya' sawed-off ol' sonovabitch," Art yelled in a testy voice. "Why you ridin' hell-bent for leather in on a feller?" As the words left his mouth he saw there was a lady with Seedy and quickly added, "Beg your pardon, ma'am."

"Please don't blame Seedy. It's my fault, I was in a hurry to see Blackwood."

A moment went by, then Blackwood, who had slowly and carefully made his way down from the ridge above camp, said, "Howdy, Seedy, don't you think it's kinda early to come callin'?" Before Seedy had the opportunity to answer, Blackwood noticed the woman. Her face was a pale oval, framed by unruly red hair. "Cora, what the devil got into you to ride out here in the middle of the night?"

"Is that the thanks I get for worryin' about you? Besides, it's not the middle of the night, it's almost dawn." Cora dismounted and stepped close to him. "All of us have been frettin'. I heard even Wilma has been tryin' to find you."

"Did you tell anyone you were comin' out here?" Blackwood asked gruffly, first looking at Cora then Seedy.

A wintry smile touched Cora's lips. "No," she answered coolly. "Maybel wanted to talk to you about staying a couple more days in Camp Precious. She said someone had seen you go into the saloon, so I went to fetch you. The first person I saw was Seedy. He wouldn't tell me where you were but said to meet him before dawn and he'd take me to you."

Blackwood moved next to Seedy and began asking questions in a low tone.

Art dropped a load of deadfall beside the campfire. "Come on, Jim, let's stir up this fire and make some coffee for the folks."

Jim grumbled, "Why don't we invite the whole town an' have a party?"

As gray streaks of dawn appeared Blackwood and Seedy sat with their heads together. Seedy was saying, "Had a bit of trouble finding all your gear. Your camp looked like a herd of cattle ran through it. Like to never found your side arm."

"I thank you for going to the trouble. But reckon you better stay out of it now and let me handle things."

Seedy waved off Blackwood's advice and said, "They've gotten so used to havin' me around to fetch-an'-carry an' clean up, they don't pay me no mind. So I did a lot of cleanin' close to the tables, while watchin' an' listenin'. The big feller those jaspers left with durin' Jim an' Art's fracas the other night is called Sandy. He's a bad one." Seedy pursed his lips and nodded. "Remember that young feller ya asked about that same night? Well, it seems no one knows where he come from, but I heard 'em call him Wilbur. That Wilbur sure do talk funny."

Blackwood stared at the fire on the tip of his cigarette, took a long pull, and exhaled. "Seedy, I don't know what's in this for you but I appreciate the information. Now I want you to back off before you get yourself in a peck of trouble."

"Seen trouble before," Seedy said dejectedly. "An' ain't gettin' nothin' out of this but the satisfaction of helpin' someone that needs me."

They measured each other. The big man saw clear eyes, open honesty, and strength in a weather-beaten face the years had not been kind to. He also caught the emphasis on the word "need" and knew Seedy was telling the truth. A shadow of a smile touched Blackwood's lips and his hand came out. "Friend, I think I understand. However, I still want you to go easy an' not draw attention to yourself."

By this time Cora had won Jim over and he had stopped grumbling. "Don't you two want some of this coffee?" she called to Blackwood and Seedy. "Guess I have to take it to them," she told Jim as she precariously balanced three cups and headed in their direction. "Lawdy me" —she handed a cup to Blackwood—"was that man put out at havin' so much company. An' did I have myself a time tryin' to talk him out of throwin' us off this place. But I finally sweet-talked him into lettin' us stay for a while." She then turned to Blackwood and spoke bluntly. "Still mad at me?"

He wrapped his arm around her, squeezed her tight, and held back a wince as his ribs let him know he wasn't ready for this much strain. "I'm not mad at you. I was concerned, an' the situation does call for caution."

"Landsakes, from all the swollen black and blue marks, not to mention the scrapes on your face, I'd say caution ain't near strong enough." Her Southern drawl was extra heavy as she looked him over with care. "Are you sure you're gonna be all right? Seedy told me what happened an' I'm hatin' to leave you. But we gotta head back soon, it's gettin' on toward sunrise."

Blackwood gave her a light hug, and assured her he was fine and would see her soon.

"Don't she beat all? An' that funny way she talks sure tickles me," Seedy said, watching her walk toward Jim and Art.

"Think it's possible you an' Cora were followed out here?" Blackwood questioned, as something in the back of his mind began to pester him.

"Well, I know we were partway, but don't nobody know these hills like I do, an' it didn't take me long to lose 'em. They won't be doggin' our trail 'cause I covered our tracks."

Blackwood was beholden to Seedy and didn't want to hurt his feelings, but he didn't have much faith in his ability to hide his trail. "When you ride out of here take the same path you took coming in and when you get a ways out turn to the east instead of toward Precious. Then I think it would be a good idea to ride a wide circle away from Art an' Jim's mine before heading back to Precious." He glanced at Seedy, and seeing his expression, hastened to convince him he knew he was competent. "I know, I know, that's what you no doubt planned. What I wanted you to know is, I'll be right behind you, watchin' your backside. I'm ridin' into Precious, 'cause if what you heard is true, an' it's the Sandy I'm lookin' for, I'd like to have a parley with him."

"Maybe it'd be better if ya gave yourself a little healing time before you took on a chore like that."

"I look worse than I feel. Don't let Cora know I'm following- you, it might make her uneasy. Soon's you're gone I'll have Art give me a hand with the saddle. That piebald—he's as easy-ridin' as any single-footer. Whoever was following you must have given up by now, so there won't be no trouble on the way in." Blackwood wasn't sure about the last statement. Seedy must have already drawn attention to himself or he wouldn't have had someone doggin' his trail. And they might still be out there trying to find him.

Immediately after Cora and Seedy left, Blackwood made his way behind the knoll, where Art had said his horse was staked out. Behind the rise nestled beneath the trees he saw two large wagons loaded with ore. As the piebald came to him on command Jim hustled forward. "Why didn't you tell me you wanted your horse? I would have gotten him for you. But now that you've seen the ore there is only one thing for me to do." Jim leveled the rifle and reached for the action.

"Jus' a goddamn minute, Jim," Art shouted and ran forward, knocking the rifle aside. "I don't know what gets into him." Art tried to smooth over Jim's behavior. "He always has a hard time figgerin' out who he can trust and who he can't."

"I don't trust anyone," bellowed Jim. "I learned a long time ago not to."

Unable to think kindly of being drawn on, Blackwood's eyes narrowed, his voice became frosty. "I don't doubt there are very few people a body can trust. But mark this down, the next time you point a rifle at me you better kiss this world goodbye."

"I'll have a talk with him an' explain some facts he don't know. He'll understand it ain't our gold you're after," Art promised.

Shooting Art a puzzled look Blackwood said, "I don't have time right now for you to make clear what it is you think you know. But I'll be back."

Chapter Thirty

BLACKWOOD KEPT THE piebald to a steady gait, threading his way among the prickly huckleberry bushes and proud stalks of bear grass. It wasn't long before he began to see he hadn't given Seedy the credit he deserved. "I'll be damned," he told himself, "if he don't hide his trail as well as any Apache." It was one of the few trails Blackwood had to read carefully or lose.

After a while the trail became clear and turned on to a deeply furrowed wagon track leading to Camp Precious. By this time Blackwood knew whoever had been trying to sniff out Seedy's tracks had given up.

Riding easy in the saddle, his mind began working on several bothersome questions. First, why had he been jumped and locked in that shack? The voice he had heard in the dark slowly materialized into a vague form. He was surprised to see that the figure was extremely slight and could not possibly be the Sandy he was searching for. Maybe one of the men that attacked him was Sandy, and knew that he, Blackwood, was on his trail, but if so why did he lock him up, and not kill him? It was unnatural.

After wallowing the thought around in his head, he knew that his being in the area for only half a day wasn't enough time to stir an outlaw band into violence. He was also sure his sharp tongue hadn't been the reason; he'd only spoken to two people, a barkeep and a swamper. Letting that thought drop for the moment his mind drifted to another question.

Why would Jim pull a gun on him? Was he only protecting his digs? And what did Art mean when he said he would tell Jim some facts?

Jim seemed regular enough even if he was a poor judge of men. In these times, when the only things you had to guard what you owned were a good rifle and a keen mind, he could understand why men lied about how much ore they took out of a mine. And it was obvious Art and Jim were doing better than just scratching out enough gold to visit the saloon, like they let everyone believe. As for the facts Art had said he knew, he'd just have to make it a point at a later time to go back to their mine and ask him.

Gnawing steadily at him was the last and most important question. If the Sandy he'd been trailing was in Precious, how could he get him to reveal the names of the other bastards on his wanted list before he killed him? For kill him he surely would—or see him dead—as he would all the sonovabitches that had attacked the Blackwood ranch.

The sun was up and a soft breeze moving the branches of the tall cedar trees made patches of shade dance across the wagon trail as Blackwood rode leisurely toward the gold camp.

Cora and Seedy had reached Precious long be-

fore him and no doubt Maybel knew by now he
was willing to stay a few more days. But he
would go see her himself to let her know there
would be no extra charges for delaying their
stay. If Cora had it straight and Maybel did
want to stay longer, it would fall in with his
plans. But if she had changed her mind, he
would induce her to stay by mentioning that the
supply wagon was due in a few days and it
might have the tarpaulin for her wagon. There
was no thought that staying in Camp Precious
was holding him back, for he now had unfin-
ished business in this territory.

A few miles outside Precious he decided to by-
pass the main trail through town and head directly to Maybel's camp. He would finish his
business with her and ride into town from the
west, hoping to gain a small edge by coming in
from the opposite direction. Also, he had the
idea that by coming in from a different direction
than Seedy, if those who were out for his hide
were hanging around town, they might discount
Seedy as having had a hand in his escape. This
was a long shot but worth a try.

He drew the piebald up in front of Maybel's
makeshift shelter, where the girls lounged and a
man could choose a woman to entertain him for
the customary hour.

Shifting in the saddle Blackwood saw Maybel's face peering at him from the open doorway
of the hut.

"Landsakes," she exclaimed as she moved outside to confront him. "If you ain't the sorriest sight I have ever seen."

Francine and Lily emerged, with Cora at their heels, saying, "Didn't I tell you he don't look none too good?"

They wore stricken expressions and clucked in alarm, as if they had never before seen a black eye, split lip, or a puffed-up jaw.

Blackwood gave them a lopsided grin that said, "It ain't nothing." But he enjoyed their fussing over him, particularly Francine, as it was the first time he'd seen her get stirred up over someone other than herself.

Maybel's loud vocal concern evaporated instantly. She started shushing the girls and insisting they go inside. Then lowering her voice to a whisper she warned them, "Make sure you don't tell a soul he's here." Looking grave she motioned to Blackwood to follow her. She led him to a clump of trees behind the shack.

"What the hell's the matter with you, Maybel? I don't give a damn who knows I'm here." He twisted his mouth and shrugged, a gesture suggesting puzzlement with a speck of contempt.

"Perhaps you would be happy if I was responsible for your gettin' another beating?"

With eyes flat and guarded, he asked, "Explain what you mean. How could you be responsible?"

"Well, it's..." She hesitated as if on the verge of divulging a secret. "What I mean is..." She faltered again, then seemed to change her mind and started over. "How do we know the same fiendish devils that attacked you before ain't on their way here, right now?"

"Next time they come they sure as hell won't catch me half asleep." Having a fair notion she was struggling with something deeper, he pressed for an answer. "Now tell me, what does that have to do with your being responsible?"

She was obviously jittery but his cool arrogance seemed to rankle her and she answered tartly, "Well, we're standing here talkin' an wastin' time, ain't we? That means I'm keeping you from getting away."

There was a stunned silence as his face turned to stone and his cold green eyes fixed her with a penetrating stare. Calmly reaching in his vest pocket for makings, he built a cigarette. After taking his time lighting it he studied her a moment longer through a cloud of smoke. "You're plumb wrong if you think I aim to run."

She raised her arms in a display of agitation and he noticed she winced. Wanting a moment to get a better hold on his temper and an excuse to change the subject, he pointed toward the wound she had received in the fight with the Indians and asked, "Does that still bother you?"

"Never mind my arm. Anyway it's fine, just has a little twinge now an' again. Let's get back to what I want you to do. Get your things together an' go on down the trail, we'll leave here come early mornin' an' meet you." She was looking anywhere but into his face.

"Like hell I will." He lifted his hat, ran his fingers through his hair, and angrily resettled the broad-brimmed Stetson. "I heard you wanted to stay a couple more days, an' I just stopped by to let you know it's awright with me."

"The girls talked about staying a while longer but that was before we knew what had happened to you. Now, I think we should get on our way, right?"

"Nope. If ya want me ridin' herd on this outfit, ya might as well settle in for a few more days, 'cause I ain't ready to leave. Right now I think I'll find a creek, clean up, and go see what's happenin' around town." He climbed in the saddle, looked down at her, and said stiffly, "I'll keep in touch."

She shrugged, a gesture of surrender. "You are undoubtedly the orneriest critter I have ever come across."

Chapter Thirty-one

THE SUN WAS riding at a slight angle, slowly settling toward the west, when Blackwood dismounted in front of the saloon. While pausing a moment to speculate on what the rest of the day might hold in store for him, he watched a famil-

iar figure staggering up the street. As the figure
drew close Blackwood held out a steadying
hand. "Goddamn, what the hell happened to
you, Seedy?" Seedy's clothes were torn and
dirty. His face was battered and there was a
large burn on one cheek.

Seedy lifted his eyes to the face of the big
man. Holding himself in tight-lipped control he
said, "While Dan was out, two bastards come in
the saloon and drug me out the back way.
Wouldn't you think one of them yellow-belly
whiskey guzzlers sittin' in the bar would have
handed me a gun or done somethin'? Hell no,
they just sat there bug-eyed and scared while
them two mongrels hauled me off to that
shack." He pointed to a dilapidated, weather-
beaten shanty, standing off from the others, at
the far east end of the gold camp. "The low-
down curs thought they could get me to tell
where you were by punchin' hell out of me and
burnin' my face." He smiled at Blackwood but
there was no humor in his eyes. "But ya can bet
yore bottom dollar they got nothin' outta me. I
was makin' a hell'va lot of racket and they clobbered me good—knockin' me down. I reckon
they figgered I was out cold but I heard 'em say,
plain out, they would get some answers 'cause
they was gonna haul me off into the woods and
really work me over. So when they went outside
to get their ponies I snuck out the back. Now
if'n ya will give me room I'll be gettin' my

rifle an' go after them dirty sons-uh-bitches."

"Not so fast. What did they look like?" Blackwood's green eyes had turned to chips of ice, his face was grim.

"One was a big Texan and the other a scrawny, pale-skinned, squinty-eyed, mean-looking sonovabitch."

"Hold on till I get back." Blackwood climbed back into his saddle. "They are bound to have hightailed it out of there soon's they found you gone. There's no hurry, we'll find them. Whyn't you go on in the saloon an' have Wa-ka-nah see what she can do for that burn on your face. I'll go have a look-see around that shack. If I turn up anything I'll let you know."

"I'd just as soon get my gun an' go with ya."

"No, I'll just take a look around while you have Dan's cook see to that burn."

"Then you'll be right back?"

Blackwood nodded and spurred the horse forward. He had no intention of coming back to fetch Seedy before he took care of the two himself. This was his problem; Seedy had helped him, and by giving that help this trouble had come to roost at Seedy's door. To spare him any more difficulties Blackwood would settle this alone.

He spent better than an hour following two riders that had split up. Then wasted more time following another trail that only circled and headed back toward Precious. After a while he decided it was a worthless effort to spend another minute pursuing indistinct tracks. There were too many fresh ones around the place to figure which was which.

On entering the bar to tell Seedy he had come up empty, two ear-splitting reports filled the small smoky room. His eyes swiftly adjusting to the dimness, he saw Seedy lying on the floor. All the customers were against the far wall but for the two Seedy had described to him earlier. These two were standing facing the fallen old-timer, each holding a smoking pistol.

His side arm still holstered, Blackwood called out, "You boys are packin', he wasn't an' that makes it murder."

In suprise the outlaws spun around, jerked up their weapons, and fired.

Chapter Thirty-two

THE TWO SHOOTERS did not have the know-how to spin and fire. They were off balance, off target; their shots went wild. All that could be seen was a silver streak as Blackwood's six-shooter cleared leather, then two more loud reports filled the room. The Texan and the squinty-eyed bastard dropped to join Seedy on the floor.

Before the echo of the shots died, Dan stepped inside the saloon. In a voice choked with rage he shouted, "What the hell's goin' on in here? Why you shootin' up my place?"

Holstering his pistol, Blackwood laid a hand on Dan's shoulder. With a trace of remorse in his voice he said, "Easy does it, Dan. Those two over there got Seedy, but as you can see they ain't goin' anywhere."

"It's so goddamn dark in here I can't see a damn thing. What you talkin' about, got Seedy?" It took a brief minute for Dan to overcome the temporary blindness and savvy Blackwood's words. "For Christ's sake, who would want to hurt an old man?" He hurried to Seedy's crumpled form.

His face shadowed with anxiety, Blackwood knelt beside the pair. He hoped his aim had been off and at least one of them would live long enough for some straight talk. He well knew these men were not the brains behind the play. But with a glance he saw his aim had run true and more than likely both were dead before they hit the floor.

Blackwood moved toward Dan but stopped as two men carrying Seedy's body crossed in front of him. He drew out a coin and dropped it in the shirt pocket of one of the men, who promptly protested, "You don't need to pay us again, Dan already paid us to take care of him."

"You keep it an' do an extra good job on a marker for him."

Blackwood stepped to the bar as Dan poured himself a shot of whiskey. He raised the bottle, made a motion to Blackwood that asked if he wanted some of the same. Knowing Dan stood to make about seven thousand dollars off a barrel of whiskey in less than a week, made it easy for him to accept. Tossing off the drink he pushed the glass forward for another. "Was hopin' one of them was still alive to answer a few questions." His fingers rolled into a fist as he pointed his thumb toward the dead Texan and his partner. "Sure would like to know where the other three are holed up."

"I saw 'em early this mornin'. They were leavin' that shed at the east end of town. Think they were headin' in the direction of them mountains behind the shack." Dan watched the cloud lift from Blackwood's face, knew instantly what he was thinking, and quickly said, "Hold on a minute, I'm goin' with you, just let me get my rifle." Dan turned, reaching for the firearm on the shelf behind the bar.

"Naw, wouldn't work. While you were gone someone would steal you blind. Better you stay an' keep watch on things." An inquisitive group that had gathered moved aside, making way for Blackwood as he headed toward the door.

Dan seemed to see the truth in this and hung back as Blackwood left.

Wasting no time getting to the shack, Blackwood made a careful search and found the tracks of the three riders heading up into the mountains. While dogging their trail for several miles through the midst of trees, down gullies, and over hills it came to him that they were still trying to sniff out the trail Seedy had used to Jim and Art's mine.

It was getting past noon and his belly was letting him know it had grown accustomed to eating a midday meal, when he came to an area where the three riders had stopped to rest. He saw they had spent a while letting their horses feed and had themselves idled away some time, the evidence being crushed grass and cigarette stubs scattered about. One of the riders had given up at this point and the other two had continued to the northeast. Blackwood found signs that the lone rider had cut to the old wagon road and was making a beeline toward Precious. He opted to follow the two riders.

The stallion was mountain grown with a fair share of bottom, but wanting him to be in top condition for whatever ordeal might unfold, Blackwood dismounted. Fishing in his pocket for his tobacco, he rolled a smoke while waiting for the pony to drink his fill from the nearby stream and take a short breather.

Hearing a rustle in the tall grass, he tensed then relaxed as a small animal bounded away, spooked by his horse.

Gazing at the sky he saw it was about three hours till dusk, and shortly after that it would be too dark to track. Gathering up the reins he was now anxious to get on with it, as he didn't relish the idea of spending a night enduring a cold camp.

Nearly an hour after being in the saddle again, a vague uneasiness tugged at him and he slackened the pace of his horse to a slow walk. He was about to nudge the pony forward when he heard an irritated bawl from someone ahead of him. Quickly dismounting, and quiet as a faint ribbon of smoke, he moved forward. Just short of the edge of a clearing Blackwood stopped. As he crouched in the shadows of the dense undergrowth he saw a rider gesturing impatiently toward the line of trees to his right.

The rider hollered, "Dammit, Sandy, get on up here or we'll never find that trail." The rider looked agitated as he jerked his horse about in the direction he was shouting. "Come on, you know the man won't pay us a damn nickel of that four hundred if we don't deliver. You're just seein' things, ain't no one behind us."

There was a rustling and Sandy broke through the brush beneath the cover of trees.

Blackwood stepped forward and in a calm and measured voice said, "You gents lookin' for something?"

Chapter Thirty-three

WHEN THE SHOCK of hearing Blackwood's voice hit them, they wheeled their horses about and went for their pistols.

Sandy let out a startled yip and frantically tried to complete his draw, but his skittish horse reared. Working to control the touchy beast he dropped one of his pistols, cussed, and grabbed for the reins. The twisting, turning animal caused him to lose a stirrup and his heel came down hard, raking a spur across its flank. The horse reared again. Sandy was still grappling for control when his excited mount lit out in a dead run into the patch of woods.

There was no chance for Blackwood to take action because the pistol grasped in the hand of Sandy's partner was coming into line.

Blackwood heard the blast and felt something strike him above the knee of his right leg. Bracing himself he grabbed his iron and squeezed off a round. The reward was knowing the rider had expended his last breath as he toppled backward off his horse.

He paid no mind to the wound or the dark stain spreading on his trouser leg. Blackwood was now operating on instinct. Hobbling back toward his horse he stumbled and fell as the injured leg gave way. Removing his neckerchief, he made a hasty bandage, struggled to his feet, and made the clicking sound that summoned the piebald. With a face that grew tighter he mounted and urged his pony forward in the direction Sandy had disappeared.

Dusk was closing in as he moved slowly and cautiously onward. Suddenly, sensing that he was not alone, his hand moved to the butt of the iron on his hip. A slight whisper of movement and a brief glint near an outcropping drew his attention. Before he could take action there was a belch of flame, then a searing pain ripped across his ribs. Rolling off his horse he slapped it on the rump. As the animal jumped forward he drew a bead on the spot he had seen the flash and got off two quick shots.

"You're a dead man, Blackwood." Sandy's yell came to him out of the gloom.

"Don't count on it," Blackwood shouted as he fed shells into his six-shooter. "It seems you know the name Blackwood. Bring anything to mind from the past?"

"Hell yes, I know the name. The weasel told us. As for the past, I ain't got no idea what you're talkin' 'bout."

Blackwood shifted his position and saw Sandy hadn't picked as good a spot to hole up as he first thought. There was a high sheer wall behind him but the low rocks in front afforded little cover. "The weasel? Who in the hell is the weasel?" he asked.

Sandy hooted. "That's the fella that's gonna

pay me four hundred in gold when I drag your body to him."

"Before you go draggin' my body anywhere tell me the names of the boys that was with you when you hit the Blackwood ranch." Directed by memory and the sound of Sandy's voice Blackwood sighted and fired again, then immediately rolled behind a runty bush. It was well he did for no sooner had he moved than lead peppered the spot he had vacated.

"Go to hell," Sandy roared. "I never laid eyes on your place."

"Don't give me that shit. I suppose you also wasn't the one that stole a big paint horse from there?" Blackwood surmised killing was ordinary to Sandy but good horseflesh might jog his memory. Cutting loose another shot, then ducking across a narrow clearing, he slipped behind the stump of a fallen tree.

"Ha! So that's the two-bit place you're talkin' 'bout? My pal Jake took that hoss an' they ain't a damn thing you can do about it. He took off for other parts," he taunted, firing a couple shots that went somewhere over Blackwood's head.

Blackwood struggled to hold back the overpowering fury that burned deep inside him. His mind raced and his eyes kept busy searching the area where he had seen Sandy's pistol spit fire. "When I was north of here a few weeks back I watched one of your pals dance at the end of a rope for trying to repeat the same play you all made at the Blackwood Ranch."

"What pal? Was it Jake?"

"Can't rightly say . . . coulda been." Blackwood hedged. As Sandy's voice had come to him from the same place each time, Blackwood had his exact spot pinpointed. He was ready to make his move, but hesitated in order to come up with something to say that would get Sandy to reveal more information.

Before he could say anything Sandy shouted, "You dirty, lyin' bastard, they didn't get Jake. He told me he was goin' south to fight 'Pachies for his uncle on the Bar H." Then flame spit from his pistol, once, twice. One shot went wild while the other hit too close to suit Blackwood and he quickly limped forward, dodging behind a shaggy pine with large drooping branches.

The light changed again. The unnatural twilight lengthened the shadows, but cast an eerie glow on the rock wall behind Sandy. His dark figure was plain to see against the large pale rock as he stood to make his boastful declamations.

With a mouth turning grim, Blackwood said to himself, "You're not very smart, Sandy ol' boy, an' a damn sight too confident." The pistol bucked in his hand as he squeezed off three rounds that delivered his message.

Sandy jerked as the bullets struck him and his hand went slack, dropping his forty-five. Clutching at his belt line he pitched forward. Blackwood managed, mindful of his game leg, to cross over and move Sandy's pistol out of reach. When he turned him on his back Sandy moaned, "I'm gut shot. Help me."

Blackwood looked at him with a cold eye. "You're gonna suffer most of the night an' be dead come mornin'. Don't see how I could get help here 'fore noon tomorrow." Wary, he sat down on a rock and studied the tree- and brush-choked mountainside to get his bearings. Spotting his pony a few yards away he summoned him. Then painfully pulling himself into the saddle he pointed the piebald toward Precious without a backward glance.

Chapter Thirty-four

NIGHT HAD SETTLED in by the time Blackwood's surefooted stallion moved onto the old wagon trail that led to the gold camp. A cool, dank wind had kicked up, stirring the debris on the trail. The vanishing light from a rising three-quarter moon turned the trees into obscure objects as it slid behind a dark cloud, then a light drizzle commenced to fall.

Blackwood rode hunched in the saddle. He was aware not only of the pain in his leg but of the blood oozing from the wound into his boot. Lifting his hand he touched his side where

Sandy's bullet had found its mark. He winced, realizing it was more than just a nick. Pulling out his shirttail he bunched and pressed it against the wound to hold back the trickle of blood.

The night grew darker as the soft rain fell from the low clouds and a smell of wet vegetation hung in the air.

Blackwood's mind touched on the thought of tracking the man Sandy had called the weasel. But it was impossible to track on such a black night and by morning the rain would have washed away all traces. But he could... Stopping himself he snorted at these ambitious thoughts. What was needed was some rest or someone to give him a hand, as he was growing weak and less coherent.

Resting his hand on the pony he softly said, "Old friend, it's now up to you," and gave the piebald its head.

The muted hoofbeats of the stallion and the trees shedding their drips of rain were the only sounds breaking the silence.

The piebald bypassed Precious, and took the unconscious Blackwood directly to Maybel's camp, finally stopping near the girls' makeshift shack.

Through a veil of mist Blackwood thought he heard loud laughter, music, and Francine singing. The din faded as a soft darkness enveloped him. Sometime later, Cora's voice came to him, brushing aside some of the fog. She was scolding him with a voice that had a catch in it. "Good heavens, look at you. Besides gettin' yourself knocked about an' all shot up, you look like a drowned rat."

Someone had carried him inside to a cot made from rough logs. Pieces of bark still clung to the logs, and a rope laced across the bottom held the straw ticking.

Maybel was working to remove the boot on his wounded leg. "Goddamn," he cussed. "What the hell you doin'?"

"Lordy, I'm sorry. Hurts like hell, don't it?" Like Cora's, her voice also held an odd tone.

Even in his semiconscious state he realized she was only trying to help. Dazed and glassy-eyed, he mumbled, "Yeah, a mite," closed his eyes and drifted off again.

Waking with a start it took him a moment to realize it must have been the quiet that woke him. The straw in the ticking crackled as he turned his head. A lamp on a box across the small room was turned so low there was hardly enough light to make out the figure of one of the girls slumped in a chair beside his bed, sound asleep. His body ached but he felt warm and dry. Instead of sinking into a dark cavity as before he now slipped into a deep restful sleep.

The rain had passed and slanting afternoon sunshine bathed the small barren shed with radiance. His eyes opened and traveled around the room before comprehension came. The bed he lay on was under an open cut-out window against the outside wall of a little lean-to off the girls' shack. His holster and guns hung on a peg near the door. Not liking them so far from hand he made a mental note to have them moved to the bedpost near his head. His bedroll lay in a corner. As his mind pieced together the reason he was laid up, the door opened and Cora came into the room.

"Well, I'm glad to see you're awake at last," she said, moving to the bedside. "It's past noon an' company is here. Jim an' Art are outside, an' first thing you should do is thank 'em." She caught his questioning look and explained, "There was so much racket around here yesterday evenin' we didn't hear you ride in. If it 'twern't for Jim an' Art comin' by last night, you would still be out yonder on the wet ground." She checked his bandages then made for the door, saying, "I'll fix some eats while you all visit."

He tried to rise. "Wait, hand me my—"

"Will you quit that fidgetin'," she broke in, "or you'll start bleeding again. Then all that patch work we did will be for naught." Cora frowned as she scooted out the door before he could ask for his guns.

No sooner had Cora left than Art stuck his head in the doorway.

Blackwood motioned him to come in. "I hear I owe you." Then he nodded to include Jim, who was on Art's heels.

Waving his gratitude aside they moved to the

foot of the bed as Art said, "Happen' to come in last night an' stop at the saloon. Dan tol' us about Seedy an' that you'd gone lookin' for them other fellers. Dan was gettin' edgy 'cause that sod-soakin' gully washer blew in an' you weren't back. We come over here to see if anyone had heard from you. By the looks of ya, ya must have run into a peck of trouble." He shifted from one foot to the other, waiting for a comment from Blackwood. When none came he gave him a probing look and continued. "It was raining bucketfuls when we found you out yonder under that big tree. Your stallion was standing over you like he was on guard duty."

"Where is the piebald?" Blackwood asked.

Art pointed to Jim. "He saw to him, he's fit."

"I had me a time with him, but I rubbed him down then put him where there's good grass an' he can get to water." Jim grinned then turned serious. "We hung around Dan's place last night, waiting to come by today to see how you was farin' before we went back to the mine. An'... there's a...Damnation, there's something else I gotta get off my mind." Jim cast Blackwood a troubled look.

"Well, go on, spit it out." Art regarded his brother with annoyance.

Jim licked his lips and started what sounded like a practiced spiel. "Art an' me had a long talk an'— Hell's fire, man"—he interrupted himself—"I had no reason to get so het up the other day an' I don't want no hard feelings."

Before Blackwood could comment Art cleared his throat and said, "We are thinkin' on sellin' the mine to a feller in Fort Boise. Our maw is gettin' on an' our little brother must be havin' it hard—with the farm an' all. We're thinking it's time we hightailed it on back and give him an' Maw a hand. Dadburnit, what I'm tryin' to say is, 'fore me an' Jim leave I thought we should talk a bit an' I'd tell you what I know about your folks."

Blackwood betrayed no emotion. "What about my folks?"

Art studied him a moment then said, "When Seedy brought you, all busted up, to our claim the other night he said you had been carryin' on about some low-down varmints harmin' your sister, an' killin' your maw an' paw. When he said you seemed to think all this happened in a place called Paloxy River Valley I knew you right off, 'cause I was there."

Chapter Thirty-five

———

BLACKWOOD'S REACTION TO Art's words was sudden rage and he sat upright. The room tilted. Gripping the sides of the bed, he held on until everything floated into place. "What say?" he asked fiercely. But in that moment he knew Art had made the statement without a trace of a thought that anyone would consider he had taken part in the raid. Calming down he asked, "You was there?"

"Hold on." Art's eyes widened. "I doubt you should be sittin'." Quickly moving forward he eased him back down. "Cora will sure as shootin' throw us outta here if those wounds open."

"Damned if she will, till I find out what you know." It was visible to all he was a lot more comfortable flat on his back. "I'll be go to hell," he said to himself, as he was forced to recognize that he would have to get used to this position for a few days.

Art cleared his throat, straightened his shoulders, and linked his hands together as he often did when he was going to do a good deal of talking. "Well, 'twas like this. I was on my way to get Jim, here." He pointed a thumb at his brother. "Wanted him to go prospectin' with me, an' we had a right smart of luck. Ol' Jim an' me was coming to—" He stopped. "Get a mite off track at times," he said and forced himself back to the story. "Anyway, as best I can 'member, I'd just come through a brush-choked draw an' up a ridge to a stand of timber. This tree-covered rise overlooked a steady slope an' the purttiest spread I've ever seen. I'd reined my bronc and was about to step out again when I saw a bunch of riders spurrin' fast away from the ranch house. I moved in a mite closer, but was still hidden by those trees," he was quick to add. "Takin' another look I saw two people on the ground, but was too far away to make out more'an that. I quick moved farther back for better cover, 'cause there was about eight men in that outfit." He paused and Blackwood asked, "That's it?"

"No." Art shook his head. "When I crouched low an' crawled forward again there was one feller hanging back trying to throw a rope on a paint horse, in the corral. I heard another feller that was out a ways shout, 'Jake, let that damn horse go an' get yore ass up here.' But that one didn't quit until he roped that big paint, then with the paint in tow he lit out ridin' like the wind to catch up. After they left I went for my hoss I'd tied back in the trees, an' went on down to the house. When I got near I saw those two people on the ground was older folks an' then I spied a young girl sprawled in the doorway. Honest to God it gave me quite a turn. I thought they all was dead so I hightailed it out of there to the nearest town to tell the sheriff. When I finally found him I'd jus' had time to say howdy when we saw you atop that wagon tearin' into town. Sheriff said he'd talk to me later and went hurryin' after you. Word spread fast about what happened to your family an' that you'd brought yore sister in to the doctor. Later I joined the posse an' we trailed that bunch of murderin' horse thieves more'an five days. Those outlaws was goin' every which way, leadin' us in circles.

The sheriff was mighty put out an' said he'd
have to handle their capture another way, so we
broke up. I'm sure sorry we didn't catch 'em,"
he ended with a long sigh. There was a moment
of uneasy silence, then Art spoke up again. "I've
always wondered why I didn't run into you on
my way into town."

"You didn't see me 'cause I was off to the side
of the trail, watering the team. When I got home
an' found my folks I remembered seeing someone pounding leather toward town, an' sometime later got the idea that that someone might
have had a hand in it." He slid a look over Art,
then continued. "I'm right glad you didn't."
Blackwood knew Art had told it straight because that patch of trees he described, overlooking the house, was the ranch's wood lot. The rest
of the tale fell in with Sandy's admission that
Jake had stolen the paint horse.

It grew clear the injured man was growing
weary. Art nudged Jim, and told Blackwood
they would look in on him again soon. After
shaking hands all around the brothers left.

Blackwood was held in the grip of dark
thoughts. Art's story had brought it all back,
fresh again. Frustration now set in at the
thought of the time it would take before he
could be up and about. He was still fretting
when the door opened and Cora came in carrying a plate of food. The aroma made his belly
growl.

After settling herself in the chair, close to the

bed, she said, "I want you to eat all this, it will help you gain your strength back," and held the spoon laden with food toward him.

"Gimme that." He reached forward. "Come on, I can do it myself. You've done enough for me." Looking into her eyes he saw a deep well of kindness. As she moved the spoon out of his reach, her color deepened. When she found her voice it was husky. "You jus' stay quiet. That bullet you took in your leg left a hole as big as your fist when it come out the other side. Dammit all, you almost bled to death. If that ain't enough, the furrow dug out of your side by another bullet almost took one of your ribs with it. And if that still ain't enough there's all those cuts, scrapes, and bruises. Mainly the bruise on your other side that's so ugly there has to be some broken ribs. So be quiet, an' chew. I'll do the feeding."

Blackwood gave in, resigning himself that come hell or high water she meant to be the one wielding the spoon. "At least let's open my bedroll so you can have your bed back. This is your bed, ain't it? And I'm piled in it is why you slept in that chair last night, right?" Opening his mouth again he took another bite of the food she offered.

"That smelly ol' bedroll ain't fit to sleep on and you ain't strong enough to get at it. Anyway, if I cottoned to wanting in this bed, all I'd have to do is nudge you over an' climb in." She tossed her head saucily. " 'Course you would likely bleed all over the place 'cause my nudging is really something." Giving him a sensual look she laughed.

"You know, Cora, you're a canny gal. I've heard it called a roll in the hay, never a nudge. But it sounds interesting—wanna give it a try?" He laughed with her, winced, and grabbed at his sides. "Damn, that hurts, so don't try any more of your humor on me." He tried to put indignation in his voice but it fell flat. Then of a mind to catch up on the news, he asked, "Tell me what's been happening. How's Lily an' Francine getting along?"

"Forever scrapping," Cora said, stuffing his mouth with another bite.

"I think they enjoy their fights. Bet Maybel's in a lather 'cause I cut short her wanting to move on?"

Cora scowled as she scraped the bowl for the last bite. "Don't think she is tore up about that but something is sure eatin' at her. Could be Wilma giving her trouble, but if we ask, she about takes our heads off. Wilma is staying in the wagon an' Maybel won't let us go near it. When she goes, she comes back crying her eyes out."

"It's not for us to judge, but I'd say Maybel has spoiled that girl." Blackwood's face contorted. Cora handed him his makings and he built a smoke.

Something in the depth of Cora's eyes said she

agreed with him. But she felt obliged to defend Maybel's actions.

"She does what any loving mother would do for her child. It's not her fault Wilma's so mean an' always takin' advantage of that love." Cora's expression was pensive.

Wilma's image flashed in front of Blackwood, then glancing at Cora he saw she was waiting for a comment. He could only nod in agreement, while something in a far corner of his mind nagged him.

Chapter Thirty-six

THE FOLLOWING THREE days dragged for Blackwood. It had been quite a stretch since he'd stayed under a roof for such a long spell. He was getting restless. He longed to be astride his horse, in the sunshine, gazing at the snow-capped mountains while taking in his fill of the fresh, cool spring air. He couldn't stay cooped up much longer. It was a sure bet the gent who was willing to part with four hundred in gold to see him dead wasn't laying low waiting for him to get well. That the gent could be close by didn't rest easy on his mind, either. Already, these days he spent in bed had been a big bite out of his time.

Slowly raising himself, he perched on the side of the bed. He'd practiced sitting yesterday afternoon and many times this morning. The dizziness had left him and now he intended to go a step farther. Planting his feet firmly on the floor he gradually uncoiled and stood upright. The room tilted. Holding on to the bedpost and bracing himself against the bed enabled him to stand a few seconds. He was stiff and ached with a constant brow-pinching pain. Gently he eased his protesting body back down. He would try again after a few minutes' rest. The goal he kept in mind was to retrieve his pistols, still hanging on the peg near the door.

Glancing sideways he saw Cora enter with the noon meal. Drawing a blanket over his hips, he greeted her. "'Bout time someone come to see me."

Staring at him she said in a small, frightened voice, "Landsakes, your face is a sickening shade of gray. On top of that you're soak'n wet. What in heaven's name is going on?"

"Nothing." Blackwood tried to look relaxed.

"Nothing, what you mean nothing?" Her words and manner showed she was on the verge of getting worked up.

"Hold on. I only been moving around some. A little sweat ain't nothing to get yourself in a state about. Besides, if you'd hang my holster on this bedpost, I wouldn't keep trying to get up an' get it."

"I told you you don't need the darn thing. But if you're gonna get yourself in a fix every time I leave the room, I'll bring them to you right after you eat this." She handed him the spoon and plate.

"'Bout ti—" A faint sound caught his attention.

Having lost her anxious tone, Cora now gained a harsh one and said, "You're the most—"

"Shush," Blackwood broke in, "an' listen."

"What is it?" she whispered.

"Thought I heard someone cry out. There, there it is again." He was sure the first cry had sounded frightened but the second held a definite warning note.

"It's Maybel." Cora jumped to her feet. "She's hollering at someone to stop. Good Lord, it sounds like they are coming right in here."

The words were no sooner out, than the door was pushed open with a loud bang.

When Cora jumped up she had moved between Blackwood and the door, blocking his view.

With a taunting laugh the newcomer said, "Finally found you. I should have looked around here first, knowing you'd be hiding behind women's skirts."

Blackwood's temper flared. "Dammit, Cora, will you get the hell out of in front of me?"

Cora moved, Blackwood took one glance and knew he should have insisted on having his pistols near him. Too late, he realized Seedy had as much as told him who was after his hide, when he mentioned how funny Cora and Wilbur talked.

Without a shadow of fear he said, "Howdy, Wilma, or is it Wilbur? It make you feel larger than life packin' an iron?"

"Wilma, is that you?" Cora looked quizzical.

"Don't call me that, my name is Wilbur. I'm not a stupid girl, I'm a man, an' you better remember it. As for you, Mr. Blackwood, it don't matter, 'cause you ain't gonna be around long enough to call me anything." Wilbur awkwardly pulled a pistol from the waistline of his breeches.

A wild look in his eyes told Blackwood that Wilbur wanted him dead and would stop at nothing to get his way.

No nonsense had ever plagued Blackwood where men were concerned and now he cursed himself for not seeing, from the start, beyond the skirt. For this oversight he was now so close to death he could almost smell it.

Lily and Francine were gathered behind Maybel in the doorway, murmuring their dismay, and shock, at what they saw.

Maybel stepped forward, taking hold of Wilbur's arm. "Come on, Wilbur, you don't want to do this. Let's go have a cup of coffee an' talk."

"The hell I don't. Why do you think I offered those bastards four hundred in gold to capture him for me?" Raising his pistol he struck her across the face as he flung her from him. "If you touch or come near me again, you'll be first to die instead of second."

Struggling to keep her balance she fell against the door frame and grabbed at Blackwood's holster to steady herself. Her hand came to rest on the butt of his Colt.

Wilbur turned back to face Blackwood, leveling his pistol. "You an' Maybel made Jenny leave. She wouldn't stay after seeing my mother act like a bitch in heat. You will die first to join all those others I had to kill. After you Maybel must die, then Jenny will come back to me."

"No," Cora cried out, "Jenny fell in love an'—"

"You shut up or one of these bullets will also have your name on it." Wilbur waved the pistol at her.

Looking at the pistol, Blackwood knew, from the position the hammer was in, it wouldn't fire.

"Maybel, give that thing ya got in your hand a fling?" Blackwood said, hoping she would toss him his firearm. He saw he was not getting through to her, so the next best thing was to buy a little time. "I didn't have a hand in Jenny leaving. She decided her own self." He saw the expression on Wilbur's face and knew this would not work. "Be damned if I'll whimper," he said to himself, then asked, "How about pitchin' me a pistol? I'll take my chances on catching it and drop you where you stand."

Blackwood heard the click of an action, then a deafening explosion filled the room.

Chapter Thirty-seven

THE ECHO OF the shot ebbed and an overpowering quiet covered the room. Stunned, Blackwood sat perched on the cot with Cora standing nearby, horror written on her face. Lily and Francine were in the doorway, shock holding them rigid. Wisps of smoke were rising from the barrel of Blackwood's Colt, which Maybel held in her hand. Wilbur was in a heap on the floor, his life's blood forming a pool around him. They stood like that for what seemed an eternity, frozen in silence.

Suddenly, a loud, mournful cry tore from Maybel's throat. She dropped the forty-five and ran to Wilbur. Gathering him in her arms she began rocking to and fro. "My darling, my son. What have I done to you?"

Word spread fast, and Dan with many miners from Precious came to console Maybel.

For several days after they buried Wilbur, on the side of a tree-covered knoll overlooking the grassy, rolling hills below, Maybel moped about. Most times she was half dressed and her hair unkempt. She lost interest in pushing on to San Francisco or in pursuing any of the plans that once excited her. When she began making noises about being arrested, Blackwood got wind of it and set her straight. He explained they were a far piece from any law, and if she was taken into custody there wasn't a judge in the land that would prosecute her.

Blackwood knew the catch-in-the-gut feeling of having another man die by his hand. The memory sickened him. But when it was a member of your close family and executed by your own hand it was a heavy load to live with. Even though Maybel had been marked to die second, she had gone to an enormous expense to save his life and he owed her a great debt.

In the aftermath of Wilbur's death many hidden facts came to light. Wilbur had been at the bottom of the troubles on the trail, as Blackwood had surmised despite having been unable to see beyond the dress. All were surprised to learn that Lily and Francine didn't actually hate each other and enjoyed their spats. Blackwood suspected Cora wasn't happy being a whore, and when he questioned her, she admitted, "I like to choose my men and not take on come-what-may." Giving him her brightest smile she then confessed to coming West with the idea of buying herself a stretch of rich farmland with a house large enough for her parents, brothers, and sisters to all live happily together.

Some while later, Cora, Lily, and Francine convinced Maybel no one held her at fault and it was time to get on with living.

To alleviate Maybel from the terrifying memory of his forty-five being used to kill her son, Blackwood decided to prepare to move out on his own trail. He was anxious to put these last days behind him.

Being a man to never back off from what he considered to be right he started by hiring Art and Jim to protect and guide the girls the balance of the trip to Fort Boise.

Early the next morning while checking the condition of his stallion, he ran his hands over him, saying, "You're getting fat, and it has nothing to do with that winter coat you're still wearing. You could do with a little exercise." After finding the pony in good shape he patted him on the rump and ambled on in search of a water hole in which to bathe.

Finding a dry creek bed that was now overflowing with melted snow water, he shivered and splashed. When he could no longer bear the cold water he began dressing. While putting on the clothes Cora had washed and mended it came to him she would make a good wife. Thinking ahead he tried to foresee what would happen. "No need to stand here an' cogitate on it," he growled out loud, for he knew life and death walked a thin line on his chosen trail. He knew he had picked a path he must tread alone and quickly put the marrying thought out of his head. He hung the fancy mirror Cora had rounded up for him in the fork of a tree and commenced to shave. Gazing at himself the thought struck him, I'm fit and it's a fine morning to ride out.

The End?

The end of a book is never really *the end* for a person who reads. He or she can always open another. And another.

Every page holds possibilities.

But millions of kids don't see them. Don't know they're there. Millions of kids can't read, or won't.

That's why there's RIF. Reading is Fundamental (RIF) is a national nonprofit program that works with thousands of community organizations to help young people discover the fun— and the importance—of reading.

RIF motivates kids so that they *want* to read. And RIF works directly with parents to help them encourage their children's reading. RIF gets books to children and children into books, so they grow up reading and become adults who can read. Adults like you.

For more information on how to start a RIF program in your neighborhood, or help your own child grow up reading, write to:

RIF
Dept. BK-1
Box 23444
Washington, D.C.
20026

Founded in 1966, RIF is a national nonprofit organization with local projects run by volunteers in every state of the union.

OUTPASSAGE
JANET MORRIS & CHRIS MORRIS

It could have been the ultimate in blind dates, but before Dennis Cox and Paige Barnett can cement their mutual attraction for each other, they are shanghaied to a backwater planet where a fermenting rebellion threatens IST's mining interests as well as the planet's existence. Drawn together in their mutual desire for truth and justice, Dennis and Paige battle the unknown in an epic adventure complete with New Age space war, politics, and spirituality.

ISBN: 0-517-00832-7 $3.50

AN INTERSTELLAR EXPERIENCE

ON SALE NOW!